THE SAVAGE GOD

THE ARES TRIALS

ELIZA RAINE
ROSE WILSON

Editors: Christopher Mitchell

Cover: Yocla Designs

ELIZA RAINE
ROSE WILSON

BOOK TWO
— OF THE —
ARES TRIALS

THE SAVAGE GOD

For all those who feel they don't belong.
Your tribe is out there.

1

BELLA

Adrenaline tingled through my body as the portal closed behind me, taking the light of Erimos with it. I blinked into the dimness, my sword raised and every muscle in my body tense and alert.

The stone tables that I had seen Joshua's body on stood foreboding and empty in uniform rows, lit by candles set in iron sconces on the walls. I scanned the cavernous space fast, counting five tables across the width of the room, and too many to keep track of stretching the length. I stood as still as I could, ears straining for the sound of anyone else in the windowless space with me but I was sure the room was as empty as the tables were. Reaching out to the closest tentatively, I touched the dark stain I'd seen from the other side of the portal.

Blood.

More tension gripped me, and I felt *Ischyros* heat in

my hand. I clutched the weapon tighter, the sensation lessening how alone I felt.

You had to leave Ares, I told myself. *You owe him nothing.*

The rage he had caused by betraying my trust surged in me, steeling my determination. I didn't need to feel guilty. The backstabbing god had brought this on himself. I was here to save my friend, and that's what I would do.

But the ache in my chest didn't lessen as I shoved the feeling of loss as deep down as I could.

I moved forward, purposefully. There were no exits where I was standing, so I needed to find one.

Checking everything around me carefully as I walked, I made my way through the tables. Any clue could be useful. I noticed that the walls seemed to be paneled in dark wood, but I saw nothing else but tables and flickering candles.

My mind raced, trying to work out how so many bodies could have been moved from this room, and where they might be now. With magic in the equation, I supposed anything was possible. Why would the Lords send me here if there was nothing to be found?

Part of me knew for certain that they didn't want to help me. This was a trap, for sure. But was their intention to kill me so that I couldn't help Ares? Or was it to give me what I wanted so that I *wouldn't* help Ares?

The former seemed the most likely, I realized, and my steps quickened at the thought. I didn't regret my decision though. If there was a possibility of finding Joshua here, wherever *here* was, then I had no choice but to take it.

Joshua was someone I did owe something to. He may not have been honest with me during the time we'd spent together, but he *had* spent all of it trying to help me. Not just using me like that giant asshole had.

I quickened my pace further. I knew I was taking less care to check my surroundings for anything other than a door or window but I didn't want to be in the grim room anymore. I wanted light, and air. I wanted to know where I was, and why. I wanted to find Joshua.

Relief washed through me when after another few minutes, the end of the room finally appeared in the gloom. I half-jogged to a dark archway set in the middle of the wall. It led to a narrow and equally dim spiral stairway, leading up and I took the stairs two at a time, the faint hope that Joshua might be at the top spurring me on faster.

I was not expecting what I saw when I burst through the wooden door at the top of the stairway.

At all.

I was on a ship. A colossal ship, with shiny wooden planks, masts like giant tree trunks, and sails...

My breath caught as I stared up at the sails that were hanging from three masts. They looked like they were made from liquid gold, sparkling metallic colors shimmering across them as the fabric rippled. As if responding to me noticing them, a huge gust of wind blew across the deck, whipping my hair up and causing them to snap taut. I wasn't sure I'd ever seen anything so beautiful.

Something was wrong though, something funda-mental, and it pulled me from my awe. I blinked around myself. There were clouds floating by on either side of the ship. Colored clouds, pastel pinks and purples, with glittering dust corkscrewing through them.

There was a distinct lack of salty ocean scent in the air, and my pulse quickened. I took a slow step out of the doorway, glancing back to see that it was set in the raised back end of the ship, a spoked wheel atop the platform above it. A vague memory of pirate movies told me that was the quarterdeck. I glanced toward the other end of the ship, some distance away but close enough to see that there was an identical quarterdeck at that end too. That was definitely different to the pirate ships from the movies.

I walked carefully, knowing it wasn't normal for a ship this size to be apparently devoid of crew. But I saw nobody as I approached the high railings, and tenta-tively peered over.

My stomach lurched, my heart starting a small stampede in my chest as I stared down at nothing but clouds. We were flying. The fucking ship was flying. Zeeva's words about flying ships pricked at my memory, and exhilaration filled me.

A flying pirate ship.

"No freaking way," I breathed, my words lost to the clouds whizzing past us.

A cold feeling blew over me, and at first I thought it was the wind generated by the ship soaring through the skies. But as my hair stood on end, and an icy trickle snaked down my spine, I realized it was something else. Something magic. Almost relieved that I wasn't alone on the ship, that there was something there that might help me find Joshua, I raised my weapon and turned around.

Shadows that hadn't been there a moment before were crawling down the central mast, and dark smoke seemed to be seeping up out of the wooden planks of the deck. A tangy smell that made me think instantly of blood rose with the misty smoke.

"Show yourself!" I called out, as red seeped down over my vision. A low, keening wail started up, distant at first, but growing in volume fast. It set my teeth on edge and made me want to cover my ears, but I kept my stance as it was, moving slowly away from the railings. I wasn't stupid enough to keep my back to a fall that high. "You don't scare me! I just want to talk."

"Talk?" A voice replaced the wail, hissing and high-pitched and seriously unpleasant to listen to. "Nobody ever wants to talk to me."

"Well, I do. Show yourself."

"You really do not have any fear of me?"

"I don't know what or who you are. So no." I was lying. I feared the unknown far more than I feared foes

I could see. If this smoke creature was the Underworld demon, then I would rather it were standing in front of me, giving me a damn clue as to how I could fight it.

The pulsing smoke and shadows whipped up suddenly, drawing together in front of the mast, twenty feet from me. I tried to keep both the awe and fear I was feeling from showing on my face as the keening started again, pitched higher, almost a shriek. The sound filled my mind with images of grief, loved ones hysterical as they wailed over corpses. A surety that I would soon become one those corpses clawed at me. There would be no one wailing with grief over my body though. I was alone. I was always alone.

A sickening desolation took me, and I almost lowered my sword arm when *Ischyros* fired to life. Warmth pulsed from the hilt of my sword through my whole being, forcing out the darkness bleeding through me. *It was the thing's power causing my fear; I had to be stronger than it was.*

But knowing that what I was feeling was being instilled in me by magic made it no less terrifying.

Wings stretched slowly from the dark mass before me, huge and dark and leathery. I focused on them, seeing that they were torn and jagged, the arches at weird and broken angles. Then the rest of the blackness melted away, leaving me a clear view of what I was facing.

I had been wrong about being less scared of foes I could see than those that were hidden. This thing should have stayed in the shadows and smoke for eternity.

The creature had the body and head of a curvaceous woman, but the damage to its wings were nothing in comparison to the rest of it. Her skin was blackened as though she had been brutally burned, the only color coming from gaping red wounds slashed all over her body, rotten flesh and bone protruding nauseatingly. Her face looked as though it had been melted, her features sagging and her mouth hanging too low, as though her jaw was no longer connected to her skull, and just her charred skin was keeping it there. It made her gaping mouth look as though she were screaming. Her eyes were worse though. They were solid black, and utterly devoid of soul, and I'd never seen anything so jarring or unnerving. Even Terror's blank features were preferable to those pits of nothingness.

"You smell like War," she hissed. Her mouth didn't move as she spoke.

I took a ragged breath. "Who are you?"

"I am not given a name in the Underworld. Who are you?"

"Bella," I said. My palms were slick with sweat, and I could feel it running down my back, despite the cool wind blowing over the ship. "Where are we? And where are the Guardians?"

"You just missed them, baby goddess." There was a high-pitched cackle, and I shuddered involuntarily. "Zeus needs me to move them often."

"Zeus? What's he got to do with anything?"

"He freed me. I do not ask questions, and he lets me have souls." Smoke billowed up around her as she said the word "souls" with chilling excitement.

"Where are the Guardians?" I asked again. My skin was fizzing with adrenaline, and I was struggling to contain my energy. Every part of me longed to lash out, to prove to this threat that I shouldn't be fucked with. It was my go-to response to fear.

"Why are you here? You smell delicious."

My stomach churned at her words. "The Lords of War sent me here. Do you know them?"

Another cackle emanated from her. "The Lords of War are too kind," she screeched, the sound making me flinch. "But I don't think my master wants me to take your soul. I think he has plans for you and the other one."

"The other one? Ares?"

"But you smell so good... I'm sure he can make a new plan."

"What is he planning?" My muscles tensed as she moved, hovering slightly closer to me. I had no idea how to defend myself against her.

"That's not my business. Why is the other one not with you?"

"I... I came alone." Saying the words felt wrong, and guilt about abandoning Ares welled up inside me. "Tell me where the Guardians are, now!" I projected as much power as I could muster into the words, and saw my skin glow in response. *Thank fuck for that.* I was seriously under-equipped in this face off. I didn't know how to fight a demon, Joshua was nowhere to be seen, and I couldn't flash.

I was stuck on a flying ship with a shit-scary demon

that wanted my soul. A bit of glowing was definitely what I needed.

A low growl rumbled across the deck, distant screams sounding on the wind.

"You know, you smell even better when you use your power," she hissed. "Like fire and steel and earth."

That's what Ares smelled like, I realized. A fierce wish for him to be at my side speared through my head, and I bared my teeth, angry with myself for being so needy and weak. But as I tried to convince myself that I didn't need the God of War's help, the more I realized just how out of my depth I was. I felt a surge of strength flow through me as my power turned the fear into anger.

"Stop fucking smelling me and tell me where the Guardians are!"

"No. I'm afraid you are too delectable to give up, baby goddess." With a piercing shriek that made pain lance through my skull and terror coil around my chest simultaneously, she swooped at me.

2

ARES

I heaved in a breath as my chest constricted, as though a vice was gripping it. I knew what was causing this latest alien feeling. It was anxiety.

I actually feared for the girl's safety. To the point that my heart wasn't beating steadily, my pulse was racing and my throat was tight. My body was betraying me, behaving like a besotted child when it should be steady and solid and immovable.

Damn this woman!

As strong as Bella apparently was, she could not face an Underworld demon alone. She had no training, no idea what she was dealing with, and no escape.

"Eris, if you care for me at all, you will do as I ask!" I barked the words as my sister sipped slowly from a metal goblet.

It had taken me nearly twenty minutes to find her after I had sprinted from the fighting pit back to Erimos, and now she knew she had me exactly where she wanted me. Desperate.

"Brother, you know I care for nobody."

"If you take me to her, I will wreak havoc," I tried. Something flashed in Eris' dark eyes.

"Well, I do love a bit of havoc," she murmured, setting her glass down on the wooden table before her. I had finally found her in a brothel, and she had refused to leave. A naked young man appeared out of nowhere and refilled her goblet, glancing nervously at me. I was still in full armor. Eris winked at him.

"Bella hates me right now," I continued. "And she will be sure to be causing trouble wherever she is. It's a win-win for you."

"The thing is, Ares, I know who is behind the Lords' new enthusiasm for taking you down. And it's not someone I want to fuck with."

"Who? Who is doing this?"

"I already told you, I'm giving you nothing for free."

Another bolt of worry clawed at my insides and I snarled before I could stop myself. This invasive, constant, useless emotion did not belong inside me, and I didn't know how to remove it, other than assure it of Bella's safety. And Eris was the only person I would ask for help.

"What do you want?"

"I want to know who she is, Ares."

"No. I can't tell you that."

And I couldn't.

Another infernal new feeling flared to life alongside the anxiety. *Guilt.* This one was becoming familiar to me now. And the two combined... How the hell did mortals get a single thing done with all this debilitating emotion churning around inside them?

"Then I can't do a thing for you, brother. It would not be worth his wrath."

I latched onto her words. "*His* wrath?"

She waggled her eyebrows at me, eyes shining. "Oops. Did I say that out loud?"

"Eris, either tell me what you know, or send me to Bella. I swear the chaos will be worth it for you."

I knew she wanted to help me. I could see the struggle on her face as she stared up at me. "Give me something in return," she said eventually.

"I can't tell you who she is."

"Then admit to me that you like her."

I was thankful that my helmet hid my face. I could feel it heating with unease, embarrassment and... *excitement*? What the hell was this collection of feelings supposed to be? Gods, they were endless! The further from Bella and her power I was, the more they invaded my being. It was untenable.

Eris laughed. "Your eyes have the look of someone who has just been caught doing something they shouldn't have been. A look I know well. That will do for now, brother." She was beaming at me and I shifted angrily.

"I have told you nothing! I tried to drain her, just like you told me to!"

My protests were pointless though. Eris' smile didn't change as she stood up. "That love-witch of yours is going to lose her shit when she finds out. I can't wait! Oh, do me a favor? If anyone asks who helped you, don't tell them it was me. Tell them it was Hermes. That'll confuse the fuck out of them."

With another cackle of laughter, the world flashed white around me.

The scene that met my eyes was both breathtaking and terrifying, and I was prepared for neither.

The sight of Bella moving across the deck of a ship faster than I could follow, her glowing sword moving like it was performing a dance just for her, was borderline erotic.

But the hell-demon swooping after her, backing away from the light of her sword, then trying to dart around it, would not tire as fast as Bella. I knew exactly what she was, and what she would do to Bella if she reached her.

"Keres demon!" I bellowed.

The demon screeched as she turned to me. Bella froze, shock on her face as she saw me, and possibly a flash of hope.

"He does not smell as good as you," the creature hissed, turning back to Bella.

"Return to Hades, at once!" I roared.

The demon ignored me completely, snapping her rotten wings out at she threw herself at Bella.

Without a second's hesitation, I drew on the cord that connected us, and flashed us both off the ship.

3

BELLA

"What the fuck was that thing?" I half screamed the question at Ares when the light from his flash faded away. My brain wanted to work out where I was and what the hell was going on.

My body wanted to smash everything.

I'd known that I couldn't beat her. I'd felt my muscles tiring, the burning ball of power inside me ebbing away, the rotten stench of the demon getting stronger every time she got closer to me. I'd known that at some point she would get to me, and I had no escape. A refusal to accept my fate had sent me into a frenzy, and my hands were burning as though they'd been inside the Hydra again, my vision blood-red.

"You fucking betrayed me!" I yelled as Ares' eyes found mine, and I knew they would be wild with rage.

"Hit me," he said.

Like the freaking Incredible Hulk, I swung blindly with my sword, roaring and yelling and swearing as it met armor with a ringing clang over and over. Heat fired through me from where I gripped the sword with both hands, each time it made contact sending shocks pulsing up my arms. And they felt good. Over and over again I landed blows on him, barely aware of my actions. I knew he was drawing my power, I could vaguely feel the cord humming in my gut, but I didn't need it.

I kept hitting him until my arms couldn't lift my blade high enough any more, and my breathing was so labored my head spun.

My chest heaved as I dropped the sword to my side, and Ares locked his eyes on mine.

The red mist ebbed away, and questions crashed through my head so fast and thick that pain throbbed at the base of my skull.

"Give me your hand," said Ares quietly.

"No," I spat automatically. He reached forward and grabbed it anyway, and I yelped in pain and dropped *Ischyros* to the ground. There were blisters on my skin. A slow pleasurable tingling spread across my skin, and it dawned foggily on me that he was healing me.

I snatched my hand back, the pain returning immediately.

"I can do that myself," I hissed.

But when I tried to concentrate on fixing the wounds, I found I couldn't, my head a jumbled mess of frustration and confusion. "I have a lot of fucking questions," I said through gritted teeth, giving up on my burns. "And if you don't answer them, I will not spend a minute more with you."

Ares stared through his helmet at me a long moment, his expression unreadable. Then with a sigh, he turned. "Fine. I'll tell you everything I know. But I'm having a drink. Want one?"

I blinked in shock at his back. I'd expected an argument. Not an offer of a drink.

"Yes. Nectar."

I was exhausted. Physically, and magically. I looked around myself, limbs beginning to shake slightly with the adrenaline still coursing through my body. We were in a room made from wooden logs. Ares made his way to a counter fixed to one wall, next to a large bookcase. The room was big and open, with a bed and closets against another wall and couches in the middle. A small kitchenette with a sink lined the wall to my left.

I moved slowly, sitting down on a pale pink cushioned couch. All the furniture looked like it belonged in a retirement home.

Ares turned back to me, carrying two glasses. He passed me one, then sat down on the other couch, a pretty coral color. If I hadn't been so angry and confused I would have laughed, he was so out of place in a room like this.

I opened my mouth to demand he talk, but he started before I could speak.

"The demon on that ship is a Keres demon. They are the spirits of violent death. They are supposed to take souls from battlefields. I do not know why this one has stolen the Guardians' souls."

"Can the souls be returned?" My throat constricted as I asked the question, Joshua's face filling my mind.

"Yes. The demon will answer to Hades when it is returned to the Underworld. He will ensure the souls are replaced."

Thank fuck for that.

"Keres demons are strongly connected to my... our power, as violent death is connected to war. I had hoped for a moment she would obey me. But she is an exceptionally strong example."

"She said she was working for Zeus," I said. "Why?" Ares froze, then took a very long breath.

"Cronos, most powerful and dangerous Titan in the world, is imprisoned in Tartarus, in the Underworld. Zeus recently sought to free him, to remind the world that Titans are dangerous. He then planned to recapture him, to prove his own dominance."

I stared at Ares. "What a dickhead. I'm assuming this history lesson is going somewhere relevant?" Ares ground his teeth a little, but continued.

"It is the belief of the other gods that Zeus was overconfident in his ability to defeat Cronos if he were freed again. The war in which he was originally captured and imprisoned was great and glorious, but it took the help of many other powerful Titans who betrayed Cronos to win."

"Titans like Oceanus?" I ventured. It had been clear when I first got here that Oceanus was more powerful than the others. He was apparently the only one who could restore Ares' power.

"Yes. And Prometheus, and Atlas. These Titans have since vanished, having been made unwelcome in Olympus by Zeus. Oceanus only returned a few months ago. Hades gifted Oceanus his own realm to rule over."

I took a deep breath. "And that upset your precious father?"

Anger sparked in Ares' eyes. "Understandably! He is the ruler of Olympus, and Hades had no right to break the rules. We are not allowed to create new realms."

"Get to the point," I said, my patience waning. I was still furious with this asshole, and I needed to know what any of this had to do with Joshua and the demon.

"Yes, it upset Zeus. His plan failed, as Hades and Persephone managed to keep Cronos imprisoned. The rest of us confronted Zeus and... You know what happened after that."

"He took your power and fucked off."

Ares exhaled angrily. "Yes, if you must be so crude about it. I don't know what Zeus would want with Guardian magic." He lapsed into thoughtful silence.

"Why would he need so many of them? There were hundreds of tables in that room." Saying the words brought a painful reminder that I had completely failed to find Joshua. I took a swig of nectar, swallowing down my shame and disappointment.

"Of course!" Ares' exclamation made me jump, and I cursed. "That is why none of the gods can find Zeus. He's using Guardian magic to hide himself!"

"What?"

"Guardians hide magic from mortals. It's what they do, they mask power. I think Zeus is using the demon to steal Guardians' souls, and then he's using their masking magic to keep himself hidden from the other gods." There was admiration in his voice.

"If what you just said is true, Zeus won't want to give up the demon. So why have the Lords of War been offered it as a prize for the Trials?"

"I do not know what connection this has to the Lords. But if Zeus has enough souls, he no longer has any need for the demon."

"Oh." I took another sip of my nectar. Ares had not touched his drink. He couldn't. His helmet was still on. At the thought of the face I knew was under the metal, fresh pain panged through my middle, a pain born entirely of emotion.

"Why did you do that to me? Why did you try to drain my power?" I asked, my voice barely audible. I dropped my eyes to my hands, unable to look at his eyes in case I lost my temper again.

"I told you. I thought it was the fastest way to win."

"You are really so selfish? So cruel?"

There was a long silence, so long that I could not help myself from looking up at him.

His eyes were filled with emotion, brimming with sadness and doubt. But as my eyebrows shot up in surprise, they drained completely, as though cold walls had slammed back down around him, dousing out his burning irises. "Yes."

My own hope was doused out just as fast. "Then I won't help you."

"If you want your friend back, you have no choice."

"I always have a damned choice," I said, my voice rising. "Always!"

But I didn't, and we both knew it. He was right. I couldn't flash, I didn't know how to get back to that ship, and I knew deep down that I couldn't best the demon alone. She was far too powerful.

Ares was right. I had no choice.

4

BELLA

Before the God of War could say another word, and I could lose my shit again, I leaped to my feet.

"Where is the washroom?"

He pointed mutely to one of the two doors in the room and I marched toward it, still clutching my nectar. I slammed the door behind me as soon as I entered the tiny space, and leaned my back against it. Hiding from the God of War in bathrooms was becoming a habit. I groaned.

I couldn't forgive Ares for what he had tried to do in the fighting pit. He had betrayed my trust too brutally. But nor did I have the commitment to hate him any longer. I'd seen his eyes when I asked him why he'd done it, and I was sure that I hadn't imagined what I had seen in them, when he thought I wasn't looking. Just as I hadn't imagined the fire, the drums, or the heat when we had kissed.

I couldn't believe that he had acted purely out of selfishness or cruelty. If he had, the coldness would have been there from the start when I looked at him, not called upon to hide something deeper when my eyes had met his. There was more to the God of War than he was showing. He *did* care. I was almost positive of it.

Maybe I was putting too much faith in one look. Maybe I just wanted him to be better than he was.

I pushed myself off the wooden door, setting my drink down on the tiny lip around the porcelain sink, and peered into what I assumed was the shower cubicle. As soon as I got close, water began raining down from the dark ceiling. With a sigh, I began stripping out of my leathers. I took a moment to heal the remaining blisters on my hands, my racing thoughts slow enough now to do so. The act calmed my anger, my wonder at being able to do such a thing too awe-inducing to ignore. I didn't even know where the blisters had come from.

As soon as I stepped under the warm water my tense muscles began to relax and my thoughts calmed enough for me to start separating facts from emotion.

By the time I had finished scrubbing myself clean, my list of "shit I know to be true" was depressing in both content and length. I'd failed to rescue Joshua. And worse, the god who had taken him, be it Zeus or the demon, was more powerful than I was. The Lords of War had deliberately sent me to my death, presumably in an effort to kill or dominate Ares.

There seemed to be no escaping the fact that Ares and I would have to work together to beat the Lords. Like it or not, the only way to save my friend was to complete their damned tests.

There were lots of things missing from my list, and now that my rage had subsided, I needed to ask more questions. I needed to find out where the hell we were, for a start, along with where the hell Zeeva was, how Ares had found me, and how I was able to do what I had done back in Pain's fighting pit. The memory of my power kicking in during the last fight had come back full-force and I had to know how to do it again. Zeeva had said I needed magic to stay in Olympus, and now I'd had a taste of how powerful I could be, I definitely wanted more.

So many questions. And I was dreading facing the man who had the answers.

I wrapped my newly long hair in a towel and dressed, downing the rest of my nectar and taking a few long breaths before leaving the bathroom. I had to give Ares the benefit of the doubt. I couldn't trust him, but if I had to work with him, I'd rather do it believing he was worth helping.

"May I have another drink?" I asked, strolling as casually as I could into the room. Ares stood up immediately, and I faltered. His helmet and armor were gone, the gold band across his forehead the only remaining metal on his body. His soft hair was pulled back behind his shoulders, the hard planes of his face only accentuated by the loose strands. His lips parted and a bolt of something totally beyond my control hit me in my core.

Don't blush, don't blush, I told myself fiercely.

Mercifully, he turned away from me, moving to the counter.

"Where are we?"

"Panic's kingdom, Dasos."

"Right. Where is Zeeva?"

"I have no idea."

I slumped down on the pink couch. "How did you flash to the ship?"

"That doesn't matter."

I rolled my eyes. "Well, someone helped you. And given what I know about your willingness to ask for help so far, it has to be Zeeva or your sister. And if you don't know where Zeeva is..."

"Fine. It was Eris." I looked at him reluctantly as he approached me, a fresh glass of deep red wine in his hand. He had a loose linen shirt on with a wide collar, and I realized it was the first time I'd actually seen him in a shirt. He'd been bare-chested or covered in hulking gold armor the whole time we'd been together.

Somehow, not being able to see the smooth skin of his chest, his rock-hard biceps and beautifully defined abdominal muscles, was worse than them being on display. *For the love of sweet fuck, what the hell was wrong with me?*

"I still hate you," I told him, as he passed me the wine.

"I know. That is why I am making you drinks like a common peasant," he scowled back at me. "That is how a person is supposed to rebuild favor, is it not?"

I stared at him. "Well, yeah, but you're supposed to do stuff like that because you want to make up for what you did, or to prove you are actually a decent person. Not tell them that you're doing it because you have to. You have no idea what interacting with normal people is like, do you?" I realized the truth of the words as I said them.

"I interact with many people," he said gruffly, sitting down on the other couch.

"Gods and monarchs," I scoffed. "How about normal people?"

"There is no such thing as normal in Olympus," he said quietly, and drank from his own glass. Ironically, it was the most "normal" thing I'd seen him do.

"You know, I think you are completely deluded," I said, matter-of-factly.

"What?"

"I think you are so out of touch with anything real, so absorbed by your godly power, that you are missing everything good in the world. Especially in a world like this."

He gave me a patronizing look. "You know nothing of this world. I can assure you, you are sorely mistaken."

I shrugged. "I will know about this world, soon. And I bet you anything you like that I'll enjoy the fuck out of it. A hundred times more than you enjoy anything."

He gave a bark of annoyance. "I am perfectly capable of enjoying things. Just not you, or this accursed situation!"

"Charming," I muttered. "So, what do you enjoy?"

He looked away from me, discomfort flickering through his eyes. I knew what he was thinking about. Aphrodite. Unease crawled through me too, and I gulped at my drink.

"The ships," he said suddenly. "I like being up on the deck of a ship."

I grasped his words and clung on, relieved to talk about anything that wasn't the Goddess of Love. "Ships! Yes. They're good. I mean, from what I saw. I was a bit distracted." I knew I was babbling, but carried on regardless. "Do all ships here fly? Why did that one have two wheels?"

"The solar sails soak up power from light, so unless it is dark they all fly. There are different types of ship, and that one was the largest class. It is called a Zephyr. It has two quarterdecks simply because it is so large." Ares seemed just as relieved to be talking about something other than Aphrodite as I did, and I couldn't help the boundless curiosity that welled up inside me.

"What other types of ship are there?"

"Crosswinds, Tornados, Whirlwinds."

"I want to see them all," I breathed. Something twitched at the corner of Ares' mouth.

"They are how people travel between the realms. Athena and Zeus have sky realms so people need to be able to fly to reach them. Most other realms are islands in the ocean. Hephaestus has a realm inside a volcano, and Poseidon's is underwater."

A longing so intense it made my chest ache was building inside me as I tried to picture what he was describing. "Are they all run by Kings and Queens?"

"No. My realm is unique for its varied kingdoms. It is also considered unusual for its varied climate, only Apollo's realm matches it for extreme weather." There was pride in his statement.

"What are the sky realms like?"

"Zeus lives on top of Mount Olympus, and wealthy citizens live in mansions built from glass that are set in a ring of clouds around the peak of the mountain. Athena's realm is industrial. It is made up of hundreds of platforms linked by bridges. She is one of the only gods who provides for every citizen in her realm, so it is over-crowded and has lots of places that provide paid work, manufacturing and such."

He was frowning as he said the words, and a pang of annoyance stabbed at me. "Do you feel no compulsion to provide for the people in your realm?"

He shrugged. "They are not my concern."

I shook my head. "You are not a ruler, Ares. You are just the owner of a very large toy." His face flashed dark, sparks firing in his eyes, but I was frustrated enough with him that thankfully I heard no drum beating in response. "There is a difference between owning land and having subjects. Just handing off the care of the people in your realm to others without giving a shit about the consequences is not ruling."

"I have never claimed to be a ruler. I am a God," he spat. "The God of War. In my realm the strongest rule, and they earn the right to rule as they please. That it is how it is, and how it should be."

"I disagree. I'm not suggesting you make Aries any less dangerous, or you remove the ability for those who are so inclined to kill each other for power, but there are plenty of things you could deal with to make it better for everyone else."

"This is about the slaves again," he said, narrowing his eyes.

"Fighting should be about glory and honor, especially in the realm of the God of War. Not loss of freedom and money."

Ares paused with his glass half-way to his mouth. His eyes focused on me, and they were still sparking, but with something other than anger now. Interest, I thought, with a frisson of hope.

"You are saying that there is no glory in winning a fight that you are forced to participate in," he said slowly.

"Yes. If you want a realm filled with glory, slavery is not the way to do it."

"I have not considered it in that way before. The feeling when I fought as a mortal yesterday..." I blushed immediately, the memory of the kiss that followed that fight impossible to shift. But Ares continued. "People would fight for that feeling alone. It was glorious."

"Exactly," I mumbled, gulping wine. "Glorious. Glory. Addictive. You'd fill the pits without taking away people's freedom."

I looked sideways at him, my cheeks still hot. He sipped slowly from his glass, clearly deep in thought.

Why was I so attracted to a man who had the mental capacity of a teenager? A smoking hot body should not be enough to cause this level of reaction when he was fundamentally a jerk.

Because you know he can change. You know he just needs to understand what he has failed to see.

I almost shook my head at the thought. I knew that people who tried to change others were always disappointed. Not from personal experience, but from the many theater shows I'd seen. People could right wrongs, become better people, sure. That was the message behind countless shows and movies.

But to change who they actually were? That wasn't possible.

I couldn't kill my conviction that there was more to Ares though. I was watching, with a front row seat, as the man considered something he had outright dismissed a few days earlier. But didn't the fact that he had never even thought about the fairness of his realm before now mean he was the worst kind of person imaginable?

My thoughts flashed to the many awful places I'd spent time in, from prison, the underground fighting and gambling rings, to the godforsaken foster homes I'd moved through. If I'd stayed too long in a single one of them, I knew who I would have become. I knew the sense of justice and the empathy instilled in me by plays and music would have been snuffed out eventually. The violence within me, the need for confrontation and victory, would have drowned out everything else if I'd not escaped those people, and those environments.

Could anybody be blamed for becoming a product of their surroundings? My salvation had been to keep moving, to limit the amount of time I spent in the places that brought out the worst in me. But Ares was a freaking God. Where was he supposed to go? How could he choose to keep better company, or none at all?

I thought of his face, alight with the euphoria of the battle with the Hydra. His power had denied him that feeling for centuries. Perhaps his power had denied him other feelings too.

Maybe there really was more to him.

Or maybe I was just clinging to the hope that my physical attraction to him could be mitigated by him not being an asshole.

We finished our wine in silence. I wanted to ask about my power, and the demon, and what we should expect in the next Trial, but fatigue had washed over me, and Ares looked exhausted too, brooding over his drink. Deciding to wait until I had the energy to annoy him into answering my questions, I stood up and stretched.

"I'm going to bed," I announced.

We both looked at the chintzy bed against the wall.

"You know that thing you mentioned about regaining the favor of someone you've pissed off?" I said.

Ares stared up at me. "Yes."

"Well, one way to make me like you again would be to let me have the bed."

He blinked at me. "But then where would I sleep?"

The man was clearly an idiot.

"I don't know and I don't give a shit."

Ares scowled at me, but didn't argue. "Fine. I shall sleep on the couch."

"Good."

I tampered down the tiny part of me that wanted to offer to share the, actually quite reasonably sized, bed. Even if he accepted such an invitation, which I didn't believe he would, it was the worst idea ever. I just wished my body would agree with my head for once.

I slept badly, dreams of fire and ringing steel rousing me regularly. I looked over to where Ares' huge form lay on the floor each time I awoke, but he never stirred. He hadn't fit on the couch, and accompanied by a lot of grunting and muttered curses had instead opted for the rug. I didn't feel the slightest bit guilty in the comfortable bed. I intended to piss him off just as much as he had upset me.

I knew what was rousing me from sleep. The Keres demon would have beaten me. And then either stolen my soul or killed me. I wasn't sure which was worse. I had come up against few people stronger than me, and none by that margin. The knowledge that she was out there made me restless.

Aphrodite using her power on me had been bad enough, along with the knowledge that she could smite me down with a look. Even Ares, who had hardly any power, had managed to put me on my ass.

I needed to get stronger. I couldn't continue to be the weakest in this fucked up game I'd found myself in, or I wouldn't survive.

"Wake up, sleeping beauty." My cat's voice filtered through my head and I sat up with a start.

"Zeeva!" She was sitting at the end of my bed, tail curled neatly around her butt. I flicked my bleary gaze at the rug, but Ares wasn't there.

"He's in the washroom." An image of Ares naked and under running water instantly made my cheeks heat.

"Where the hell have you been?" I snapped at Zeeva, rubbing my eyes.

"You and Ares needed some space to work out your differences," she answered coolly. I raised my eyebrows.

"Bullshit."

In a heartbeat, Zeeva grew, her whole body glowing teal and her eyes a blazing amber. A lion-sized cat towered over me and it was all I could do not to shrink back under the covers.

"Do not swear at me, Enyo." Her voice rang fiercely in my head, just as intimidating as her big-cat form.

"OK, OK, calm down," I said, holding both hands up. "Sorry for swearing at you." Slowly, she shrank back down.

"I did not know where the Lords of War had sent you, but I sensed your magic when you returned and came straight here. I listened to your conversation with Ares about the demon and the ship, and relayed it to Hera. I have been here with you since."

"Oh," I said. "Well, erm, thanks. But if you're hiding from me, you can't really blame me for thinking you've just abandoned me." I couldn't help the whiny note in my voice. It was one thing to suspect that your stuck-up pet didn't like you. It was another to suddenly be able to communicate with them and find out that they actually don't. And that they can kick your ass.

"I did not want to interfere with your reconciliation with Ares."

I snorted. "Reconciliation? Hardly. The man is an-"

She cut me off before I could finish the sentence. *"Bella, you are getting through to him."*

"What?"

"He considered your words last night, instead of dismissing them. I believe his lack of power has awakened something in him, and you can take advantage of that."

I cocked my head at the cat. She was confirming what I had hoped, that he was at least capable of changing. But... "What do you mean by take advantage?"

The cat swished her tail, her eyes boring into mine. *"Tell me exactly what happened on the ship,"* she said eventually.

"Only if you give me coffee."

"Tell me," she repeated, and I rolled my eyes and pushed back the covers. I told her everything that had happened as I dressed, and she pushed me for minute details. By the time I was done reliving the memory of being completely useless, and so close to Joshua but failing him, I was mad again.

"It is as I thought. Ares saved your life."

"What?" I stared at the cat.

"He rescued you from that ship, and must have traded

something with Eris for her help. You would probably not be here if it were not for Ares."

Zeeva's words smacked into me like a hammer. How the hell had it not occurred to me already that I owed the brutish God of War my life?

My simmering anger instantly swallowed the budding guilt though. "He saved me because I'm his only source of power, no other reason than that."

"I would not be so sure."

"Do you know something I don't?" I asked her, pulling my hair into a knot on top of my head and using a band from my backpack to secure it.

"A great many things."

I gave her a sarcastic smile. "No doubt. I was referring specifically to Ares."

"I have suspicions. None I may act on or share."

"As usual, thanks for nothing," I muttered.

"You will thank me eventually," she said.

"Hmmm. I want to learn more magic," I told her, putting my hands on my hips.

"Good. But there is a limit to what I can teach you. I do not wield power like yours."

"War magic?" She nodded her feline head. "Ares isn't going to help me."

"He might."

I pulled a face. "I don't want his help."

"Don't be such a child." I bared my teeth at her before I could stop myself, but the sound of the washroom door opening prevented her from berating me further.

Ares walked into the room, wearing full armor, minus his helmet. He nodded at Zeeva. "I see you are back, now that the action is over," he said. Despite the fact that I had felt exactly the same about the cat's untimely absence, I leaped to her defense.

"What Zeeva does or doesn't do is none of your business," I said haughtily, then marched past him into the washroom.

When I emerged, I was surprised and delighted to be met by the smell of coffee.

"Zeeva said you like this muck," scowled Ares, holding out a large mug. I took it from him, inhaling deeply. I'd felt the tug of him using my power while I had been in the bathroom.

"Did you go and get this just for me?" I asked. Ares nodded. "Thank you. I could get used to these 'regaining my favor' gestures, especially if they all involve wine and coffee."

Ares nose wrinkled, and the expression was distinctly ungodly. I couldn't help a small smile.

"Coffee is rare in Olympus. It is expensive and unpleasant."

I barked a laugh. "Coffee makes the world go round."

"Not Olympus."

"Maybe not, but it's a necessity in my world."

Ares opened his mouth to answer, but I didn't hear the words.

An awful creeping cold moved over the back of my skull, and my vision went pitch black. I cried out, dropping the coffee and fisting my hands instantly.

"Little Bella has lots of lovely war magic," whispered a delighted voice, deep inside my head.

"Who's there?" I yelled the words aloud, alarm gripping my whole body at the invisible threat. How could I fight something in my head? Remembering Zeeva's training, I pulled on my power, trying to build a wall around my mind. Nothing happened.

"Calm down, baby goddess. It's just your friendly Lord of War, Panic."

I took a great gulp of air. The demon had called me baby goddess. Anger seeped through my body. "Get the fuck out of my head." More cold slithered down my neck, a feeling like a large band of ice was being wrapped around my head taking over. My vision was still dark but flames flickered at the edges.

"I'm just dropping in to tell you that the Trial announcement will be in half an hour. Ares knows where you both need to go."

In an instant the tight band of ice was gone, and the room appeared around me again as my vision returned to normal. Ares was staring at me, tight-lipped. I took an unsteady breath.

"That was one of the Lords," he said quietly.

"Yes. Why is it so different to when Zeeva talks to me in my head? Everything went dark and my head went weirdly cold." I put both hands to the side of my head, half expecting my hair to feel icy. It didn't. "Why couldn't I block him out?"

Ares glanced at Zeeva, now sitting on the rug beside him. "You are getting stronger. And you share power with the Lords of War. As long as you are in my realm, anyone who has the power of war will be able to communicate with you. Now that your power is growing, you are becoming visible to them."

"Woah, what? What do you mean, I *share* power with the Lords? You said our power was different to them, that they had specific, shitty powers." I tried to keep the worry from my voice but failed. I did not want to be connected in any way with the fucked up creepiness the three Lords had. "If getting stronger means turning into one of them, I'm out. I don't need that in my life."

"I said their power was created by mine. As with all the demigods and deities of my realm. It is not the same, but it connects us all."

"And I'm becoming visible to all of them?" I blinked, mind racing and anxiety building. I could hear my voice rising.

Ares looked at the floor briefly, before taking up my gaze again. "Yes."

I shook my head slowly. "I'm turning into a fucking beacon for your crazy war offspring, and they can make my head cold and my vision black whenever they like? I didn't sign up for this." I had begun pacing without realizing, shaking my head fervently.

"Calm down, Bella. You can learn to block them out." Zeeva must have projected the words to Ares too, because he looked down at her.

"Yes. The cat is right. You can learn to block it. And they are not my offspring. They are not of my loins."

"Who the fuck says loins?" I knew it wasn't the right question to yell at him, but I was pissed again. I hated the feeling of being one step behind everyone else all the time, too ineffective to make a difference and at the mercy of those stronger than I.

Which was apparently everyone.

"Loins are-" started Ares, but I shoved him hard in the chest. He didn't move, but he closed his mouth.

"I know what loins are, goddammit! I want to know how to stop being so weak!"

"You are not weak." Ares said the words with such simplicity that my juggernaut temper stumbled.

"But everyone has more power than me. They can get into my head, and flash me around, and make me feel stuff, *steal my fucking soul*. Everyone in this whole damn world can do more than I can, there's probably an endless amount of magic shit I don't even know about yet. I can't do any of that."

"Wrong. You can do all of that and more, and you're not even at half-strength. You just don't know how to do any of it yet." Zeeva's voice was level and soothing.

"Teach me." I sent the demand into the room in general, not caring which of them answered. Both knew more than I did. There was a long pause.

"I will teach you to keep your mind secure," said Zeeva eventually. I flicked her a grateful smile, then planted my gaze on Ares.

"And you? Will you teach me to use my war magic?"

His eyes dropped from mine before he answered. "No."

Anger spiked through me, quickening my pulse. "Why not?"

When his eyes met mine again, the fire danced in

his irises, his dark pupils endless against the mesmerizing flames. "As long as I am by your side, you do not
need to use your power."

"I'm not your damn puppet," I growled. A distant
drum beat loudly in my mind.

"And I'm no fool. If you learn to use your power, you
will not need to help me."

The drum beat again, and again, and the smell of
smoke and grass washed over me. "The best way for me
to get Joshua back is by completing these tests. I'm not
going anywhere."

"You already left once."

His words ricocheted through my head, and the
drums beat louder and faster in my mind. There was
emotion in his face that I didn't recognize, I realized as
the flames in his eyes leaped higher. Was it betrayal?
Was he hurt that I had left him?

The Ares who presented himself as stoic, emotion-
less, get-the-job-done, could not possibly mention the
fact that I had essentially abandoned him to whatever
fate the Lords had planned for him. But the Ares before
me now had fire sparking in his irises and I knew the
flames weren't fueled by anger. I knew his anger now,
and this was something else.

Whatever it was, I was now a hundred percent sure
that I hadn't imagined the look on his face the night
before. There was more to Ares than pride and anger.

My eyes moved to his lips of their own accord, and
heat flashed through my whole body, settling below my
butterfly-filled stomach.

"I won't leave you again." The words came out

almost as a whisper, inaudible to me over the rising drum beat, readying my whole being for action. What kind of action, I didn't know. But I was becoming desperate for anything.

Ares took a step back, and the drums quietened. He took another step, his chest heaving under his gleaming armor. The farther those flaming irises got from me, the more distant the drums sounded. Disappointment rocked through me, dousing out my excitement with an unpleasant dose of reality.

Ares didn't want me. And I had just told him I wouldn't leave him. Embarrassment coiled through my stomach, and my cheeks burned.

"I will teach you to fight with a sword."

His statement cut through the heavy atmosphere and I took a breath, burying my arousal and shame as deep as I possibly could with a fierce determination. I clearly needed another word with myself, but I'd be damned if he saw how much he affected me. I would deal with this stupid crush later, alone.

"A sword? How will that help against the demon or war people fucking with my head?"

"Please, stop swearing." He used the word *please* so softly, it took me by surprise enough to elicit a mildly apologetic eye-roll. "I'm offering you training in sword fighting, or nothing. Take it or leave it."

I gave a growl of frustration, but we both knew what my answer would be. "Fine."

"Which Lord spoke to you?" He abruptly changed the subject.

"Panic. He said that the Trial announcement would

be in half an hour and you know where to go. Though I guess that was ten minutes ago now."

Ares sighed. "It will be in his throne room. Zeeva, you have twenty minutes to teach her to block unwanted communication. I am going for a walk."

"A walk?"

"Yes."

"Where?"

He gave me a hard look. "Outside," he snapped, then rammed his helmet onto his head and stamped toward the large cabin door. I got a glimpse of deep green foliage on the other side as he stepped through, before he slammed the door shut again.

"Zeeva, do you hear drums when Ares gets mad?" I asked, turning to the cat.

"No, Bella. No, I do not."

6

BELLA

I t turned out that trying to build a wall around my mind as Zeeva had taught me before had actually been the right thing to do. Only, blocking out people connected to my power required a bigger, better wall. I didn't feel at all like I'd had enough time to practice when Ares returned from his walk.

"Tell me about Dasos before we go?" I asked him as he stamped into the cabin. He didn't look at me, but he did answer my question.

"It is a forest realm. Filled with traps and unpleasant creatures. Much of it is derelict, and the citizens live in fortified homes amongst the trees."

"Why do they live here at all? It doesn't sound very friendly."

"Panic pays his citizens a monthly wage."

"Just for living here?"

"Yes. Each year the households that have lasted the longest get to compete for prizes."

"Weird, but fair enough," I said, shrugging. "What's the longest anyone has lived here?"

"Eight months."

I blinked. I'd expected him to answer in years. "Oh. So... It's quite dangerous here then?"

Ares finally looked at me, through his helmet eye-slit. "The feeling of panic is a powerful weapon. It causes people to make very bad decisions. Fatal decisions."

The warning in his words was clear. Trepidation rumbled through my chest. "OK. I got it. Don't panic. Don't make stupid decisions." When it came to Ares I felt like I was the freaking queen of stupid decisions, but I didn't need to share that.

Panic's throne room looked like it had seen better days. Much better days.

I turned in a slow circle, staring at the crumbing stone walls around me. I had visited castle ruins in the north of England very similar to what I was looking at. The circular room was massive and the ceiling so high I couldn't really see it properly. Vines and creepers spread across the pale, broken stone everywhere I looked, and the air smelled damp. A breeze whistled through cracks in the walls and I rubbed my arms as the hairs rose.

"This place is a dump," I muttered, eying the only furniture in the room; a large stone chair and iron dish in front of it.

"Isn't it?" Panic's voice rang through the empty space, and with a flash, the three Lords appeared before us. "I only use it for formal occasions," Panic smiled at me. "My other castle is much nicer. If you ever want to see my private rooms, please do let me know." His eyes darkened as he stared at me and I narrowed mine back at him.

"Hard pass."

"Shame."

Terror stepped forward, his marble feet loud on the old stone floor. "How did you fare with your demon?" he asked me, black patterns swirling across the surface of his featureless face.

"You know damn well how I fared," I spat. "Why are you working with her?"

"She can offer us something our once mighty leader can't," said Terror, with a small shrug.

I felt the pull of Ares anger in my gut.

"And why is she bothering with you?" the God of War asked tightly.

"We have something she wants," Panic sang.

"What?"

"As if we would tell you," smiled Pain.

"Is it us?" I asked.

Terror gave a soft chuckle as the other two snorted. "Baby goddess, we already sent you to her on a platter. If it was you two she wanted, she would already have you."

"You will regret your lack of respect toward me." Ares' voice was low and menacing and when I felt the pull in my stomach, I released my hold on the cord connecting us just a little. My lips parted in reluctant appreciation as his skin flared to life with a gold glow, and power rolled from his gleaming armor.

I dragged my eyes from him in time to see a tiny look of doubt pass between Pain and Panic.

"That's a risk we have opted to take," said Terror smoothly.

"No risk, no reward," added Panic, his trademark smile back on his handsome face.

"You had better pray that your risk pays off. My punishment will far exceed your potential reward."

"One is not living, if one does not fear death," the Lord purred. Ares stiffened.

"Let me assure you, you will welcome death by the time I am finished with you." The warrior god boomed the threat, and everyone in the room except Terror instinctively stepped back. Even me.

"Panic, shall we proceed with the announcement?" Terror changed the subject without hesitation, dismissing Ares completely. A low rumble began, and the pull in my stomach intensified. Making a quick decision, I released my hold on my power, letting Ares take it.

The room filled with the sound of ringing steel and the tangy scent of blood. Ares grew twenty feet tall before I could take in what was happening. Raw, unconfined power emanated from him, dwarfing the creepy vibes that rolled off the Lords of War.

"I partake in these tests of my own volition. You do not control me. You worship me." Ares' voice was magnified and carried images of death so strong I could see nothing else. Battle fields, old and new, coursed through my mind's eye. I saw men in furs with huge broadswords that severed heads from necks with roars. I saw ancient warriors in metal plated armor buried in showers of arrows. I saw green helmeted men in breeches praying as shells dropped from the sky before everything was consumed by fire.

When the visions of war ebbed, I saw that all three lords were on one knee before Ares. A fatigue washed over me, and with the tiniest sideways glance, Ares shrank back down. My vision closed in a little, dizziness threatening to take me, and I heard Zeeva's voice in my head.

"Focus on your well of power. Steady yourself." I felt for the burn of restless energy under my ribs, and found it depleted and tiny. It was still fierce and hot though, and I concentrated on it, a feeling of pride buoying me. Ares had used my power to do that. They had been right, I *was* getting stronger. And if Ares could do that with my power... Could I?

Well done, war magic. You did good, I told the remaining little ball of power. My vision cleared, strength seeping back through me.

"Panic, the announcement, if you will." Terror's voice had lost its silky smoothness, a tight anger in his tone now.

Panic moved to his throne, avoiding looking at Ares, and the iron flame dish sprang to life. White hot flames leaped up, before giving way to a gentle orange flicker. A mirror image of Panic appeared in the flames.

"Good day, Olympus," he beamed, all trace of his

run-in with the God of War gone. "I am pleased to host the second test of the Ares Trials. Ares and Bella will be facing a little quest. They must find the fighting pit hidden deep in Skotadi, the most dangerous area of my kingdom. Once there, they must defeat a dragon, by plucking no less than three scales from its body."

A dragon? My jaw hung open.

Nobody had mentioned dragons. Trepidation rolled through me and I tried to dismiss it. Surely a dragon couldn't be much different to an acid breathing Hydra? We'd defeated that and survived. Just.

"We shall send the heroes off in style, with a small ceremony in one hour. Until then, farewell."

The iron dish fell lifeless again as the flames died.

"How do I call Eris?" I said, staring at my Guns N' Roses t-shirt with a frown. "I don't think I'm supposed to go to the ceremony in this." We were back in the tiny cabin, and in an effort to distract myself from thinking about the upcoming Trial, I was trying to get ready for yet another pointless ceremony. But the closet in the cabin was empty, and all I had to wear was what was in my backpack.

"I have not been able to contact my sister since we returned." I looked sharply at Ares, where he was sitting on the peach-colored couch.

"Really? Should we be worried?"

"No. She answers to nobody." I didn't doubt that.

I blew out a sigh. "Any ideas on what I should wear, Zeeva?"

The cat looked up from where she was dozing on the bed, her sleek body curled into a small ball. I resisted the urge to go and pet her, as I had for years before. It was too weird now that I knew what she really was.

"I can probably borrow a headdress from my mistress for you. But as for clothes, I can't help."

"Oh, thank you," I said. I hadn't actually expected her to offer anything. She stretched slowly, then vanished in a puff of teal light.

"I too, would like to offer my thanks." I whipped round to Ares at his words, even more surprising than Zeeva's. His helmet was off, his hair loose around his shoulders. And the way he was looking at me... "You willingly allowed me to use most of your power to intimidate the Lords. That means... a great deal to me."

I shrugged awkwardly. "It means a great deal to me too. They deliberately sent me to a demon-y death, and they're all dickholes. They deserved taking down a peg or two."

"Has your power replenished yet?"

I felt inside myself, already knowing that the burning ball of energy was full and ready to go. "Yes."

"Good. That means we did not reach your limit, and you are indeed growing in strength."

"So that was a successful experiment in sharing power?" I said tentatively.

"Indeed."

"So... Can you teach me to use it better?"

"No."

I threw the t-shirt down in annoyance. "Why not? I'm trying to prove to you that I'm not working against you! Show me how to do something useful! How did you make all that war stuff happen?"

"It's what I do. I invoke the power of war."

"Show me."

"No."

"Then show me how to grow."

"No."

"You're an asshole." Ares got slowly to his feet. The single, booming beat of a drum sounded loudly in my mind, and just that one sound sent tingles through my body in heady anticipation. With some alarm, I realized that I was beginning to crave these moments. The aching that spread through me, settling in a delicious desperation, was far from unpleasant.

There was a small flash of teal and Zeeva appeared, a gleaming gold tiara before her.

Ares sat back down.

"This should be enough to make it look as though you've made an effort," the cat said dismissively, then curled back up on the bed.

"Thanks," I mumbled, and picked up the tiara. It was beautiful, made from fine gold and set with a wavy row of tiny sparkling rubies. "I hope it goes with black t-shirts and khakis, as that's all I've got."

7

ARES

I could not help but admire Bella's confidence as we arrived in Panic's glade. The mossy ground moved under her heavy boots as she immediately sought out a serving satyr, and I saw the raised eyebrows of the other, immaculately dressed, guests as they took in her casual, very human, attire.

She didn't need a dress to look beautiful though. The gold headband Zeeva had given her glinted over her braided hair as she tipped her head back to take a long sip of her drink, and her t-shirt hugged her chest as she moved. An ache I knew was utterly inappropriate pulled at me.

She had left me. Walked through that portal knowing I couldn't beat the Trials and win the Trident without her. And I had deserved it.

I had deliberately tried to take all her power, knowing how much she would hate me for it. In fact, I'd taken her power exactly *because* she would hate me for it, but instead of severing this all-consuming bond between us, it had only solidified my feelings for her.

Whatever connected us went deeper than my burning physical attraction to her. Her excitement was infectious, and I found myself longing to see her smile. How could one person take so much pleasure from the world around her, when she had been treated so unfairly? More blasted guilt trickled through me.

Even her unending questions were annoying me less, and I was finding myself in possession of a reluctant respect for her tenacity. She was desperate to learn how to get stronger, and that resonated within me. I knew she wouldn't give up, just as I wouldn't in her position.

Sighing, I watched her wave enthusiastically, then make her way over to the white centaur she had become so enamored with. At some point, soon, I would have to teach her more about her power. She was becoming strong, and she was right - she would be a lot more helpful in getting this abomination of a gameshow over and done with if she could use her magic properly.

But what if she decided that she didn't need me anymore? Worse, what if she found out who she really was and what I had done?

The thought of her leaving again caused a lurch in my stomach that brought actual queasiness with it. *You just don't want to lose access to your power again,* I told myself. But I knew it was a lie.

Crushing the knowledge that it wasn't just her

power I didn't want to be without, I tried to focus on something else. Something that wasn't her.

With a plan forming in my mind, I strode over to where Hermes and Poseidon were talking in quiet voices. The glade was large and completely covered by thick canopies of foliage. Tiny fairy lights danced amongst the greenery, giving the place a hushed, ethereal feeling. I couldn't see any of the Lords of War.

"Ares," Hermes nodded as I approached. He was in traditional ancient clothing, his plain toga contrasting with his glittering winged sandals.

I nodded back at him. "How goes the search for Zeus?" I directed the question at Poseidon.

"I fear your father is as strong as he ever was. We can not find him."

"Do you have any ideas of his plans?"

"There is unrest in the mortal world, and my concerns for Hera are growing. But the Underworld is secure now, and he has not approached any of the other Olympians."

As if they'd tell you, I thought. Poseidon was not our ruler. But I spoke politely. "Is Hades here? I have new information that will be of interest to you both."

When Hades joined us and Hermes was dismissed, I told the brothers what I had learned of the Keres demon, and my suspicions that Zeus was using Guardian magic to mask himself. When I was finished, cold fury was rolling from Hades in long tendrils of smoke.

"I will create a new level in Tartarus to house that demon when I get hold of her," he hissed. "One she can share with my brother."

Poseidon looked to me. "We appreciate you telling us this."

I bowed my head. "I wish to help."

"And regain your power, no doubt." Poseidon did not trust me, and I did not blame him.

"Indeed. But I shall do that by fulfilling Oceanus' quest. I will leave finding my father to you two."

I walked away before they could ask me anything else. I was uninterested in how they would react to my information. I had meant exactly what I said, that my focus was on these damn Trials. Besides, I did not believe for a moment that they could stop Zeus. There was no more powerful god in the world, and all my focus had to be on regaining my own strength before my father made his move - whatever it would be. I would not, could not, be left unguarded when that happened.

I wandered around the glade talking to whomever I passed, with a forced confidence and pride in my voice. I was not going to let anybody think that the Lords had me under their control. If I behaved as though I had instigated the Trials myself, or at least that I was enjoying them, then the Lords lost the upper-hand.

I pulled very gently at Bella's power, and I felt her respond. A warm river of strength flowed through me, and I took just enough to give myself a sense of divine presence. Enough that the other gods would feel it.

"Well, well. Somebody's cheerful." Aphrodite's sweet-as-honey voice washed over me. I felt my insides melt a little, a desire to make her happy swamping my thoughts. But I drew more power from Bella, and the feeling lessened. Aphrodite raised an eyebrow as I turned to her. "She's getting stronger," Aphrodite said, her smile not reaching her eyes.

Her skin was the color of onyx today, her large eyes jet black too, and her lips were as scarlet red as her floaty, sheer dress. She looked like a painting or a piece of art. Breathtaking. "You look beautiful," I said, overly formally.

"Thank you." She didn't mean the gratitude. I could feel her annoyance. "She made a fool of you in the last fight. I thought I would find you more rage-filled than this." Her perfect eyebrows drew together in a frown. "Are you now a wolf without fangs *or* claws?"

Indignant anger leaped to life at her words, but as I opened my mouth to defend myself, a thought bore into my mind, in a voice that I was sure belonged to me, but had been absent from my brain for a very long time.

She doesn't love you.

It was the part of me that had always known that Aphrodite didn't love me, but that had I refused to believe because when I was under the influence of her power, the screaming insatiable restlessness was quieted, just for a while. It was the voice inside me that centuries of never getting enough, never finding the thrill, never reaching the point I knew I was destined to reach, had silenced. The voice that had been replaced by a louder one that led to an unending cycle of pushing the limits of everything around me, all other things in my life unimportant when compared to trying to reach that climax, that place where the thrill and adrenaline peaked, and bliss took over.

I had convinced myself that Aphrodite was the key to that feeling I craved so hard. But she wasn't. Her love was temporary, and weak and false. Aphrodite didn't want to make me better, or stronger. But Bella...

A realization crashed into me, as clear as crystal.

I would take the thrill of fighting the Hydra with Bella over a night in Aphrodite's bed without hesitation. Bella made me better. She reveled in the moment, thrived on the adrenaline, gloried in victory. When she was strong, I was strong. And she wanted the people around her to have strength; she wasn't cruel or greedy.

Something must have shown in my eyes, because Aphrodite's face began to change in front of me, snapping me from my epiphany.

"Ares, you forget who I am," she hissed, a darkness filling her eyes that had nothing to do with their color. The Goddess of Love had a wrath more vicious than any other Olympian, and uneasiness skittered through me. If Aphrodite got even an inkling of my feelings for Bella, it was not my safety I feared for.

"I don't know what you mean," I said, trying to keep my face clear of any of these new emotions. It was not something I had needed to practice in my life, and I prayed I was successful.

"I have power over love," she whispered. "I know when two people are attracted to one another." Her mouth was a hard line.

My heart stuttered in my chest a little. I drew on my pride, and tried to think of what I would have said before I lost my power, before these infernal emotions had begun to cloud my thoughts. "Bella is young, and mostly mortal. I believe she has a crush on me." I filled my words with prideful arrogance.

"And you, my warrior prince?" Aphrodite's tone changed again. Now it was low and husky, and my vision narrowed to her sensual mouth, my body reacting instinctively. "Who do you have a crush on?"

"I do not suffer from crushes."

"Prove it. Prove your love for me. If you ever want to lay your hands on my body again, do not touch her."

Before I could speak, Bella's voice called across the glade. "Aphrodite? I wanted a quick word, if you have a moment."

Fury flicked through Aphrodite's eyes, but vanished as she turned to Bella.

"That's an unusual choice of outfit. But at least you're not pretending to be something you are not." There was a sneer in Aphrodite's voice, and defensiveness leaped to life inside me. I clamped my mouth shut.

"Yeah, thanks. Look, I wanted to tell you that I have no intention of causing you or your asshole boyfriend any issues. Once I've got through these Trials and saved my friend, you won't see me again."

Bella's eyes flicked to mine. I swallowed the pang in my chest that accompanied the force of her words. She was right, one way or another. Once the Trials were over and her power was fully restored, it was impossible for us to see each other again. But she didn't know that.

She was choosing to tell me that she was leaving after this was over.

"You are not significant enough for me to be concerned about your future plans, little girl. I don't care." Aphrodite purred, then turned her back to Bella, facing me again. I expected anger or arrogance from her, but I was almost sure she looked worried, just for a heartbeat. But then she turned on her brilliant smile. "Come, mighty one. Let us converse with our own kind." She led me by the elbow toward Dionysus and Apollo, at the far end of the glade.

I let her lead me away, and it took more strength than I knew not to look at Bella as I went.

8

BELLA

I 'd been stupid to interrupt their conversation. And my announcement was totally unnecessary. But I hadn't been able to help myself. A totally irrational surge of jealousy had taken me when I saw Ares' eyes darken and his posture relax as that witch purred to him.

I hadn't even known what to say when I marched over there, and all I had achieved was being belittled in front of Ares. And now he had gone with her, like a puppy on a leash.

I ground my teeth. At some point real soon, I was going to have to find a way to stop caring. A way to stop this desire for the warrior god. Because so far, no matter what he did, it was not lessening. I was seeing more and more in him that called to me.

I looked around the glade, trying to find something to distract myself. Nestor, the warrior centaur and by far the coolest creature I'd met in Olympus so far, had been called away. Although she might have made that up to get away from my constant questions about how she fought with her war-hammers.

"You seem bored, sweetie," the goddess of Chaos' voice sounded in my head.

"I'm supposed to be able to block people out now!" I exclaimed aloud.

"Ancient deity, remember? You'd have to be about ten times stronger to block me out."

"Where are you?"

"Around."

"Why aren't you here in person?"

"I may have upset a few too many people."

I snorted. "Why doesn't that surprise me? You know, I could have done with your help in the closet department."

"Not at all. I like this look. Besides, you're about to start your Trial, and that would have been a pain in the ass in a dress."

"What? How do you know?"

"Sweetie, I know a lot of things. I know some things that would interest you a lot more than when the Trials are starting."

My heart skipped a beat. "Things about me?"

"Uhuh. And about my baby brother."

"And what do you want from me in return?"

"When I have a trade in mind, you'll be the first to know. Good luck."

"Wait!" But she had already gone. I stamped my foot, not caring how petulant I may have looked.

Everybody knew more than I did, even about *me*. It was infuriating. I was a pawn in a game a bunch of other people were playing, and I was losing patience with it.

"Good evening!" Panic appeared in the middle of the glade, with an over-the-top flash of red light. A hush fell over the guests as he bowed low to each of the Olympians, then nodded his head at me. "Ares, Bella, please. It is time to start your Trial."

So not everything Eris said was untrue. The Trial really was beginning now. I fingered my flick-blade in my pocket as I stepped forward. Ares moved too, toward the Lord of War.

"Find the fighting pit and the dragon, and get three scales. You may not flash at any point. Enjoy." He winked at us both, then we were flashed out of the glade.

The forest smelled bad. Really bad.

"What the..." I could feel my whole face wrinkle in disgust as I looked around myself. The air was heavy and damp, and there was so much foliage above us that only streaks of misty light illuminated our surroundings.

The trees were huge, as big as redwoods I'd seen in pictures before. But their branches started much lower, just a few feet off the ground, and the mass of leaves growing from them were a weird color, as though someone had sucked most of the vibrancy from them. I turned in a slow circle. A low whooping sounded some-where in the distance, and there was a constant rustling of creatures in the damp fallen leaves littering the mossy ground.

There was no path, or clearing, or any indication at all what direction we should be going in. I looked at Ares, standing out absurdly in his gold armor.

"The smell is rotten vegetation and dead animals, I believe."

I pulled a face. "Gross."

"Use your healing power. Create a thin veil across your ability to smell."

"Really?"

"Yes."

I tried to do as he described, and to my delight, the stomach-churning smell lessened. "Thanks."

He ignored my thanks, and I felt a tug on my power. "What are you doing?"

"Sensing for a dragon."

"Oh. Good idea."

I pulled my blade from my pocket as he stood unnaturally still. "Time to play, *Ischyros*," I whispered to the sword. With a delicious pulse of heat, the blade morphed in my hand, until I was holding the epic steel sword.

"There are lethal creatures everywhere in this forest. The desire to kill is all around us. I can't tell where the dragon is."

A shiver ran down my spine. "You can sense for stuff that wants to kill us?"

"Yes."

"Show me how?"

"No."

I twirled my blade in my hand, taking a deep breath. "Fine. Then which way do we go? Preferably without running into the things that want to kill us." The truth was though, I was ready for a fight. Aphrodite had gotten me fired up, and nervous energy was racing around my body, making me restless.

"I think that the strongest sense of danger is that way." He pointed to a tree that looked the same as every other tree, then stamped toward it. Drawing his sword, he hacked at the low branches, until he'd made a rough hole large enough for him to push through.

"Toward the danger it is," I muttered, and followed after him.

Hacking away at branches seemed like an abuse of my sword's true potential, but *Ischyros* did as good a job as a machete would have. The stuffy heat of the forest was becoming oppressive, the gloom just as suffocating. Alien noises were our constant companion as we forced our way through the dense undergrowth, sharp thorns and scratchy branches catching on my clothes.

"Panic is an asshole for making us go straight from the ceremony. I don't have my armor, or my backpack. And if I tear this t-shirt, I will make him pay."

"Is there anyone you don't think is an asshole?" Ares muttered ahead of me.

I thought for a moment. "Not many people, no."

Ares was silent for a while, then spoke quietly. "You

said you would leave once you have retrieved your friend. What do you plan to do?"

His question surprised me, and also caused me an irrational surge of pleasure. *He cared.* "Erm, I'm not really sure."

"Will you stay with him?" His voice was curt and clipped.

"Joshua?"

"Yes."

"I don't know." And I really didn't. "All I know is that there's no fucking way I'm going back to London. Or the mortal world."

"You wish to stay in Olympus?"

"Of course I do. I've spent my whole life not fitting in and knowing with certainty that I'm not in the right place. Olympus is everything I didn't know I needed and missed from my life. I mean, a world where it must be impossible to get bored... That's a dream come true."

Ares had slowed, and he turned to look at me over his shoulder. He had a strange look in his eyes, and I wished I could see the rest of his face.

"What?" I asked him. He turned away. "Ares, what aren't you saying?" I could feel his discomfort.

"Be quiet. I can hear something."

"Bullshit! You just don't want to-"

"Bella, silence!"

He had tensed, his sword raised and his head tipped back. Adrenaline immediately flooded through my veins as I realized he was serious.

I concentrated, straining to hear something. I felt a little rush of heat fire out from the well of power under my ribs, and it was suddenly as though my senses were amplified by a hundred. Every crack of a twig, Ares' measured breaths, even the barely-there breeze, sounded loud and clear in my ears. The muted color of the forest around me came to life, and I caught the bright colors of tiny bugs and the flash of opalescent feathers in the trees that I'd missed entirely before. Unfortunately the rotten smell hammered harder at my defenses, but it was small price to pay.

Before I could tell Ares how utterly awesome this new experience was, a loud buzzing reached my ears. I turned warily in the direction it was coming from.

"What's that noise?" I whispered. It was getting louder.

"If it is a swarm of oxys then we must defend ourselves, now." There was a note of urgency to his voice that he did not normally have, and I snapped my eyes to his. "Bella, we can't fight these easily. If they sting you, you'll have about three seconds to heal your-self, or it will be too late." He gripped my arm, and sparks of electricity shot across my skin. "I'm going to teach you to create a shield, right now."

"OK," I said, a bit breathlessly.

"Draw on your power and picture a shield. A real shield, that you would be willing to use in battle. If you do not believe that what you have imagined could defend you in a real fight, then it will not work."

"Got it," I said, and tried to picture a shield. With a jolt that felt almost physical, a massive circular metal disk flashed into my head. It was beautifully engraved with an image of two rearing stallions, spears and javelins flying behind the riderless horses. A pattern ringed the shield, and looked Celtic or Viking in style.

There was no way I'd invented this shield. I *knew* it was real.

I didn't have time to ask Ares about it though.

The buzzing suddenly surged in volume and Ares crouched down, the plume on his helmet tipping back as he cast his eyes up. I followed suit, holding the image of the horse shield firm in my mind as red seeped fast across my vision, replacing the vibrancy that had been there moments ago.

The buzzing grew so loud I could hear nothing else over it, even the rushing of blood in my ears. But I couldn't see anything in the trees above or around us.

"Where are they?" I yelled at Ares.

"This is Panic's forest; his creatures will try to incite panic before attacking." I caught enough of his words to work out what he had said, and I took a deep breath. The tactic was working. The longer we waited for the threat to appear, the more my imagination built up the foe.

I wouldn't say I was panicking yet, but I certainly didn't want to wait any longer to see what we were up against.

9

BELLA

S omething small, bright and freaking fast darted
out of the trees toward me.

I felt a slight resistance as it crashed into an invisible barrier a foot above me, then flew off into the tree again. My pulse quickened, and everything around me began to slow as my war-sight kicked in. I felt Ares pull on my strength, and I let go of a little, allowing him to take it. The next oxys that sped toward us was moving just as quickly as the first, but my power allowed me to focus on it enough to see it properly.

It was like somebody had taken a wasp and put it through a Frankenstein machine. It was as large as Ares' closed fist, and its body looked like it had been stitched together out of lots of bits of bright leather. A glowing purple stinger jutted out of its rear end, and it had hairy black wings that beat hard and fast. I couldn't make out eyes on the thing, but it had multiple furry legs hanging down under its tube-shaped body.

It smashed into an invisible wall around Ares, then flitted off.

The buzzing paused, then roared, and my stomach tightened in apprehension as a swarm erupted from the trees. They weren't just around us, they were above us too, blocking the faint light with their sheer mass. I braced myself, and felt my whole body being pushed into the dirt below me as they crashed into my protective shield. It had formed a dome around me, and a sense of being closed-in swamped me as they beat at it, covering it entirely, leaving me in near darkness. I waved *Ischyros* uselessly at them from where I crouched, taking deep breaths and wishing desperately that I knew how to make light.

A weird sense of urgency took over my mind abruptly, and I felt Ares' presence pressing at my thoughts. The second I pictured him, his voice sounded in my head.

"I'm going to create a fireball. And I need a surge of your power to do it."

He wasn't exactly asking for permission to use my power, but he was telling me beforehand, which was a significant improvement on the last Trial. "OK."

I felt a hard pull in my gut, and I didn't fight it. The buzzing upped in pitch into an awful cacophony, then the darkness was suddenly gone, a roaring inferno of orange and scarlet washing over my dome instead. The oxys scattered, the terrible sound of their buzzing fading fast.

I stood up warily as the flames died down and the

sensation of being so close to the heat but not being able to feel it was strange.

"The ground and foliage are too damp to catch," Ares said, standing up beside me. Fire licked up an invisible barrier around him too.

A few lingering oxys zipped toward us, but retreated fast as they neared the flames. "They will keep coming," Ares said. "In a few hours, they will forget that we have fire and try again."

"This shield thing is cool," I said, reaching out to touch it. My hand moved straight through the magic boundary.

"It is a useful power to have. The oxys sting is lethal."

"So if they stung me I'd have three seconds before I died?"

"No. Their sting does worse than that. It will send you permanently mad. You will become a rabid shell of a being."

I was instantly much more afraid of the oxys than I had been thirty seconds ago. "Why the hell didn't you tell me that before?"

Ares looked at me and shrugged. "I didn't want you to panic."

"Great."

"Speaking of lethal, your power is strong enough now that I think that it's safe to assume that your immortality will have manifested."

"Wait, what?"

"It's not wise to test it, but I believe it would take something extremely rare or strong to kill you now."

"But I thought demigods weren't immortal?" I could feel how wide my eyes were as my heart galloped in my chest. "Only proper gods were?"

Ares stared at me, the flames around us now dying, and the buzzing all but gone. "You are not a demigod."

"Then what the fuck am I?"

"I told you. You are the Goddess of War. We should drop our shields and save our energy."

I didn't tell him that the second he'd said I was immortal I had totally forgotten about my shield. "Immortal as in - I can't die?"

"That is the definition of immortal, yes."

"Well, fuck." The sheer implications of living forever were too massive for me to comprehend. A cascade of possibilities and fears rushed through me, and Ares turned back in the direction we'd been traveling, raising his sword to start hacking at branches. "Wait! You can't just drop that bombshell and carry on!"

"I thought you had realized this already."

"Hell, I can't even do a fraction of what you can, of course I hadn't gotten to thinking about being immortal! Who else in Olympus is immortal? Does that mean if I fall in love with someone who isn't immortal I'll have to watch them die, like in the Disney Hercules? What if I get like you and I lose the thrill of fighting?" The concerns and fears tumbled from my lips, and I surprised myself by how much they were dominated by worry.

Surely being immortal was a good thing?

But it didn't sit right with me at all. What was the

point of anything if it was infinite? How could you live in the moment, if the moment lasted forever?

I didn't *want* to be immortal.

"We need to find this dragon. Keep moving."

I did as he said, but only because I was too distracted to argue. I stepped in his wake, allowing him to clear the path for us as I tried to get to grips with the idea of not dying.

But I couldn't. It was just too... impossible.

"I don't think I can deal with this," I said to Ares eventually.

"Deal with what?"

"Immortality. It's stupid."

"I told you that you have the power of a goddess and that you were getting stronger. How is it you are only considering this now?"

"In case you hadn't noticed, the last few days have been pretty fucking hectic for me, armor-boy. I was concentrating on my magic; I didn't realize not dying came with the package."

"Immortality is the most coveted thing in all Olympus," he said, whacking at a cluster of huge leaves.

"Well, I don't want it. Knowing that you could lose everything makes you treasure what you have all the more. I know that from my shows. People who take everything for granted lose the ability to experience true happiness, or gratitude."

Ares paused, then resumed his hacking. "I have never met anyone like you," he said, quietly.

"Ditto," I answered. "What about the demon?"

"What about her?"

"Well, if I'm immortal, what's the point in fighting her? Nobody can win."

Ares slashed at the particularly thorny tangle of branches that had been behind the leaves. "She steals souls. That would be much worse than dying. She could keep your soul in perpetual torment."

"Is taking their soul the only way to kill an immortal god?"

"There are many ancient artifacts that can harm an immortal, even if they can't be killed. And some very powerful gods who have been granted the right to rule, like my father, can remove your power."

"And therefore remove your immortality?" I asked. Ares nodded. So, Zeus stealing Ares' power must be worse for him than I thought. His father had made him mortal, and removed the protection on his life. "You dad is a total douche."

"What is a douche?"

Suppressing a snicker at the thought of explaining the answer to that question, I answered him vaguely. "Mortal word for asshole."

"Why not stick with asshole? It appears to be your favorite word."

"I've decided to reserve it just for you," I told him.

He glanced back at me, and though I couldn't see his mouth to confirm that he was smiling, there was definitely a glimmer of amusement in his eyes.

10

BELLA

We slashed our way through the forest for another hour or more, and I filled the time by avoiding thinking about immortality, and practicing turning on the thing with my senses that I'd accidentally discovered I could do. I opted not to mention it to Ares, and instead silently marveled at how I could project my amplified hearing and vision at will toward noises and sights that interested me.

I was listening intently to the thud of the warrior god's heart beating in his chest, when the ground beneath my feet gave way.

A shout of shock left my lips as I plummeted downward, grasping at thin air. Before I could get over my surprise enough to pull at my power or do anything useful at all, my back slammed into something cold and hard with a splash, and then I began to sink. I'd fallen into water, I realized, my vision red in reaction to the pain and shock, but my usual focus not able to compete with my thrashing panic.

"Bella!" I heard Ares roar, and I cried out as I kicked my legs, trying to right myself, but I could feel something coiling around my thighs and hips. My head cleared the surface and I dragged in a desperate breath of air before I was tugged back down again.

I had *Ischyros* in my hand and I slashed blindly under the water with the blade, but the grip on me didn't lessen, the weapon not connecting with anything. I couldn't see clearly, my thrashing causing the murky water to bubble up, but I thought it looked like a tentacle. I kept kicking as hard as I could, and my head broke the surface for another brief moment. I saw a gleam of gold before I went under again.

Ares was in the water with me.

"Stay calm!" His voice was an urgent command in my head, and I thrashed to get to the surface. *"You can breathe underwater."*

"No," I gasped, before I was yanked back under the surface again.

"Yes. You are immortal."

But panic was winning. I was a fighter, not a contortionist. I was trapped and I couldn't get free, I couldn't breathe. I was getting dizzy, and I could feel my strength lessening as the thought of drowning overwhelmed me.

"Stay calm!"

The water around me was cloudy but I could see Ares' bright red plume through it clearly. A painful burn in my chest screamed for air and I tried to kick up to the surface. But something pulled at my legs, and I was jerked further down.

I was going to drown. I was trapped. My lungs would fill with water and I would die.

Huge black dots drifted across my vision as my legs stopped kicking, the thing coiled so tight around them now that I couldn't move.

"This will hurt, but you will survive. We need your power, Bella. Stay conscious."

Ares' voice was calm and soothing in my mind, and I clung to it, as the last few bubbles of air escaped from my mouth. My chest burned as I turned my head slowly, trying to find his eyes, to focus on something other than the darkness invading my vision. I felt a pulse of pain through my head, and I felt Ares grip my hand, the one holding *Ischyros*.

"Don't let go of the sword. Whatever happens." I was tugged down again, the light from the surface fading. My body gave in to the pain in my chest.

My mouth opened, and I inhaled, with no control over the action at all.

I don't know if I screamed as the freezing water filled my mouth, burning all the way down my throat. I was vaguely aware of the grip tightening on my hand, my weapon becoming too heavy to hold alone as blinding pain took my chest. I squeezed my eyes shut, aware of how close I was to passing out as the agony tore through me, every instinct in my body begging to shut down, to escape.

But I refused to let go, refused to give in to the temptation. Ares said I had to stay conscious.

Just as I was sure I couldn't bear the agony any longer, a rush of cool air seemed to fill my lungs from nowhere, and I choked, expelling water from my throat that burned like acid. My eyes flew open, and I gasped down more air as I realized that it was now almost too dark to see, we were so deep.

I was breathing under water.

Despite the dark, I knew Ares was still there with me, his hand still clamped around mine. As I spat up more water I tried to orient myself, and realized that the thing coiled around my legs was now up to my waist. I felt for it with my other hand, recoiling when I touched a slimy tentacle. I could feel the power under my ribs burning hot, and I drew on it, trying to send some healing tendrils to my raw throat.

"Ares?" I sent the thought to him, saying it aloud too, my voice instantly lost to the water.

"Cut the tentacles with your sword."

His mental voice was weak and strained, and fear for him rushed through me. Something was definitely wrong. *"Are you OK?"*

"Cut them." I felt his hand loosen from mine, freeing my weapon.

"I can't see where they are." After a second, a faint glow illuminated the cloudy water. It was Ares' armor. I couldn't see his eyes, but the gold gleam was enough that when I looked down I could see the purple tentacles wrapped around both of us.

Without hesitation I brought my weapon down. As soon as my blade met with the limb, the thing began to thrash, Ares and I flying through the murky water in its grip. I responded, the red mist tingeing the gold light as my blade met its mark over and over in a frenzy of movement.

I got Ares free first, only a second before severing the last tentacle with a hold on me. I immediately began kicking for the surface, only pausing to see that Ares was following.

He wasn't. I pulled my legs up and did a one-eighty in the water, heading down instead of up. Energy was racing through me now, all of the panic turned to determination.

Ares' glow was fading, and fear caught in my throat as I realized he was moving deeper into the water. The tentacles were nowhere to be seen, thank god, and I swam down after him faster.

"Ares!"

He didn't answer me, his glow almost vanishing as he sank faster. If he stopped glowing completely, I would lose him down in the darkness. New panic swelled through me, and I propelled myself through the inky water after him.

As I laid my hand on his arm, his light went out.

Power flared in my chest, and I knew instinctively that whatever Ares had been using had just returned to me. I had all of my power now, I was no longer sharing it. Which meant Ares was unconscious.

Swearing in a continuous stream of curses, I kicked upward, pulling the dead-weight that was the God of War with me. But he was heavy, and we were so deep, and I was too slow. I knew I wouldn't get him to the surface in time if he had stopped breathing. How did

the immortality work if he had no power or was unconscious? Would he survive? Why was there no fucking
manual for this?

Anger and frustration surged through me, and with
it a blessed hit of strength. My legs seemed to grow as I
swam, and a glimmer of hope pushed me further. I
drew on the burning heat inside me, willing myself to
get bigger and stronger, to reach the surface faster.

And I did. I felt myself getting larger, each kick of
my legs more powerful, Ares getting lighter in my grip.

When I burst through the surface of the water I half
threw Ares out of the pool and onto the forest floor,
scrambling out onto the mossy undergrowth after him.
Heaving for breath myself, I rolled him over, tipping his
head to one side and trying to press on his chest to
force the water out. But his armor was solid, and I
couldn't get his chest to move. I pulled his helmet from
his head, revealing his paper-white skin. Desperately, I
pressed my hands to his face and I pulled on my power,
trying to force it into him through our contact.

"Take my power," I whispered, my throat raw.
"Please. Please open your eyes."

Water spilled suddenly from his mouth and he
rolled to his side, nearly causing me to let go. But I kept
my grip on his face, pouring my healing power into him
as relief swept through me. He coughed and choked up
water as I muttered about everything being OK, and
after what felt like an eternity, he looked up at me.

His breathing was ragged and there was an intensity
in his dull eyes as I pushed his wet hair back.

"Are you alright?"

"I am alive," he croaked. "Thanks to you."

Slowly, I let my hands drop from his face, and he moved to sit up. "What happened?" I asked him.

"I... I couldn't take enough of your power without harming you. You needed it to survive the panic."

I stared at him. "You gave up the power for me?"

He looked down at his hands, then stood up, stumbling a little. "It was the only option for us both to survive." His voice was brusque, and he wouldn't look at me as he began banging his armor, getting the water out of it. "If I lost consciousness I knew you'd have enough power to get us both free. If you lost consciousness then you couldn't have saved me. By the time you came around, I would have been dead."

His words were true. I was the one with the power; without me he had nothing. I was the logical one to have saved. But his awkwardness said something different.

The man acted on pride and impulse, and had demonstrated barely any self control in a fight. So for him to stop himself from taking my power and allow himself to be rescued by me... This was definitely a side to Ares I hadn't seen.

11

ARES

My throat and lungs burned with a feeling I had not experienced in centuries, aside from briefly during the fight with my father.

Pain.

Damn my mortality! When Bella was stronger, I would be able to share her power more effectively. Wouldn't I? What would happen if we couldn't both use it to escape death?

An uneasy feeling crawled down my aching spine as I turned away from her. It was true that it had made no sense to let her lose consciousness. I would surely have perished.

But that wasn't what had driven me to let go of her power. That wasn't what had been going through my mind when, for the first time in my memory, blackness closed in around me and very real death had loomed large.

The only thing that had been in my mind, was to

save her. Feeling her terror as she thrashed and fought for her life had caused an instinct I didn't know I possessed to take over. She needed all of her power to breathe underwater, to use her immortality. And I had let her have it without hesitation. Why?

Why had I done that?

The power she held over me was becoming dangerous. That was the closest I had ever come to death, and I had put my life in her hands. She may be my most deadly adversary.

I turned a fraction, trying to get a glimpse of her without her noticing. She was standing with her back to me, her hands on her hips, surveying the forest. Her blonde hair hung wet to the small of her back, and I was beset by an image of her stripping out of her clingy shirt. She was taller, I realized, and the muscles in her calves and biceps were larger than usual. Her power had helped make her strong enough to drag me to the surface, and I wasn't sure she had even noticed.

If she was to be the death of me, I did not think she was aware of it.

"I think I know where the dragon is," she said, and I turned away before she saw me looking.

"Where?" I stooped to pick up my helmet.

"There's a distinct lack of birds in that direction."

I took a long breath, then rammed my helmet on my head and faced her. Her eyes caught mine, and I could see concern flash in them, before she looked to where she was pointing.

"Yes. That is where I sense the most danger," I nodded. "How do you know there are fewer birds?"

"I can hear them. Or rather, not hear them."

She was beginning to learn to use some of her powers on her own, which meant I would not be able to avoid teaching her to control them. "You realize you have grown taller? In order to preserve your power, you should shrink back to normal now."

She looked down at herself in alarm. "Shit. You're right. I'm almost as tall as you." There was a wonder in her voice that I instantly wanted to hear more of. Or be the cause of. "How do I shrink?"

"Just will yourself to be normal."

She snorted, raising one eyebrow. "Normal? Fuck that. I've never been normal in my life. Now is definitely not the time to start."

I couldn't help my small smile, but she couldn't see it behind my helmet. "You know what I mean," I said. "As you were before."

She closed her eyes, and started to return to her previous size with a faint gold glow. When she opened them again, she did a little twirl. "I'm going to be good at this magic shit. I can tell."

"Why do you think I'm refusing to teach you anything?" I answered, and immediately regretted the teasing comment. But instead of launching into a tirade of questions and demands, she just shrugged one shoulder.

"Looks like I don't need you to teach me anything. I just saved both our asses on my own. And I know where the dragon is."

Indignation rolled through me. "I'm an Olympian. I

could teach you things you didn't even know were possible."

"Armor-boy, literally everything in this world is impossible to me. That's hardly a bold claim."

I crossed my arms. "Infinity would not be long enough to teach you everything I know."

"Oooo, who's a clever boy?" Her grin was doing something to me. Something unexpected and inconvenient. "Go on then. Teach me something nobody else could."

With a rush of unexpected desire, my head filled with ideas of what I could teach Bella that had nothing to do with war or fighting.

The connection we shared must have translated my thoughts, because the second my eyes met hers, fire leaped to life in her irises. A drum sounded in the distance, slow at first, then louder and faster, as though my own heartbeat was setting the pace. Bella stepped forward, her eyes alive, and her lips parted.

My hands moved to my helmet before I could stop them, and as I pulled it from my head Bella let out a breathy sound. My body came alive at her response to me, desire replacing all other thoughts as I dropped the helmet to the ground.

I took the last step, closing the gap between us, and her hand came up to my face at the same time mine moved to hers.

"You saved me," she whispered, and the flames were filling her eyes, fierce and hot and irresistible, the drums of war beating around us.

"And you me," I breathed, and then her lips crashed

into mine, and the godforsaken forest around us vanished.

All I knew was her taste, her heat, her passion. Our tongues moved together in a dance more erotic than I had ever experienced, and my mind filled with a desperation to feel every part of her body against mine.

She moaned softly as I broke the kiss, trailing kisses down her jaw, her slender neck. She pushed her fingers into my hair, her nails leaving trails of tingling pleasure across my skin.

I wanted her. And it was more than just her body I needed. She was mine. I knew it, with a sudden and almost painful clarity.

She was mine.

"Ares." I froze as I realized the icy voice I had just heard in my head was not Bella's. "It is one thing to ignore my command. It is another to do it in front of the world."

12

BELLA

"W-What's wrong?"

Ares had frozen beneath me, one second his hot, hungry mouth on the sensitive skin on my neck, then the next as still as a statue.

"We are being watched." His voice was strained.

I could hear the blood pounding in my head, and my desire was so intense that my whole body felt like it was on fire. But I crouched and picked up my weapon from where I had dropped it, trying to concentrate on the threat. This was one of the most dangerous places in the world, I reminded myself, trying to block out the bliss Ares' kiss had instilled in me. We'd already been attacked by oxys and a monster octopus or some shit. Kisses could wait.

I didn't want to wait. I wanted everything Ares had, and I wanted it more than I'd ever wanted anything. I hadn't even known desire this intense was possible.

"Where?" I whispered. "I can't see anything."

"The Trial is being watched. By the whole of Olympus. I have just had a message from one of the gods."

I turned back to him slowly. "Aphrodite?" I asked, through gritted teeth. My unspent passion was turning fast to rage.

A female voice hammered into my mind, almost painfully loud. "You seek to mock the Goddess of Love?" Aphrodite's cold voice felt like a whip across my skull, and I felt myself wince. "You will pay for this. You will both pay." A searing pain tore through the base of my head and down my neck, leaving me gasping in agony.

"Bella!" Ares was crouching before me, cupping my face in his hands as black dots drifted across my vision.

"I'm OK," I wheezed. "Fuck, that was painful."

"Use your magic, heal yourself." His voice was almost tender, a tone I didn't even know he was capable of.

"The pain's gone now. What did she mean?" I straightened slowly, blinking around.

"I think Aphrodite just tried to curse you."

My stomach clenched tight, fear and anger coiling through me. "What?"

"We need someone that knows about her magic to confirm it, but I'm quite certain we have made an enemy of her."

I looked up at his beautiful face, pinched and angry. And flushed. He wanted me. I had no doubt at all. You couldn't fake a kiss like that twice.

Tentatively, I sent a thought to him. "As soon as we are alone, we are finishing this."

His eyes locked on mine, and for a second the hunger in them was so predatory heat rushed back to my core. But he didn't answer me.

Instead he ducked down, scooping up his helmet and putting it back on. *Ischyros* heated in my hand. This asshole had rendered me unconscious in front of the world, and now he had turned down my sexual advances in front of them too. Red seeped into the edge of my vision.

I opened my mouth, ready to tell him in no uncertain fucking terms that if he was still into Aphrodite, a woman who treated him like shit, that he had better not lay another fucking finger on me, but he spoke first.

"After you." He gestured into the forest.

"You are a trophy to her. Is that what you want?"

A wave of heat rolled from him as I felt a tug in my gut. "Either I hack this forest apart, or you do," he hissed at me.

I bared my teeth at him, raised *Ischyros*, and brought the sword crashing through the nearest bunch of tangled branches.

Once I started, I couldn't stop. I poured all my pent-up energy, all my desire for Ares, fear from nearly drowning, confusion about fucking everything, into the blade, and slashed and hacked with reckless abandon. I wasn't even sure if I was cleaving a path, or just tearing up a chunk of shitty forest.

"Bella, stop." I was panting as I wheeled to face Ares, god only knows how much later.

"Why?"

"The oxys are coming again."

I sent my senses out and snarled as I heard them. "Good. I'll knock them out of the fucking air." I wielded my sword like a baseball bat, and Ares grabbed my arm.

"Bella, if you are stung there is no recovery. You will live trapped in a world of insanity your whole life."

I lowered my arm. His words were serious enough to snap me out of my sword-wielding rage. "Fine. What do we do?"

"I can sense something below us. Something dangerous."

"More or less than the oxys?"

"I don't know, but it means there must be a passage or caves or something similar underground. We might be able to keep moving somewhere the oxys can't get to us."

It took us less than a minute to find a cave mouth hidden by the dense foliage, but that was plenty enough time for the buzzing to double in volume.

We barely got inside the cave before it was loud enough that I could barely hear my own thoughts. Together we heaved as many loose boulders and rocks as we could find over to the entrance, praying the oxys didn't work out that we were behind the tangle of undergrowth hiding the cave.

I had the distinct sense that we might be making a massive mistake, trapping ourselves inside a cave we knew contained something dangerous. But the oxys were the immediate threat, and we could only deal with what we could see.

"You're going to have to teach me to glow," I said, blinking in the gloom.

"Think of something that gives off a lot of light."

"Like the sun?"

"Yes. I think of solar sails, on a ship."

I thought about the colossal sails on the mast of the demon's ship, like liquid metal gleaming and shining.

"Good." I looked down at Ares' grunt, and felt a smile stretch across my face. I was glowing gold.

"You glow when you are using a lot of power," I said, looking up at Ares. He was giving off a faint light too. "Do you do that on purpose?"

"No. It is just what gods do."

I remembered my skin glowing after I'd used my power to move so fast up the hundred-hander's body. "What gods do," I repeated. "I'm an actual god. Goddess. Deity."

Ares didn't say anything, but turned away from our makeshift barrier and started to head further into the cave.

"You know, you are the worst person to have an existential crisis, or an epiphany around," I said, following after him. "Being a freaking glowing gold goddess would be a lot more fun if I had someone more impressed to share it with."

"All gods glow. It is not impressive."

"Well, I'm impressed. With myself. Not you. Your glow is shit."

He looked over his shoulder at me and I gave him

the finger with a sarcastic grin. He shook his head. "Glowing or being a goddess does not make you any less crude," he said.

"No. Seems not."

The cave was wide and cool, and I sent my new super senses out, straining to hear for anything dangerous or interesting. There was a soft scuttling sound, but it was far away, and I couldn't associate the noise with anything obvious. We walked for what I was sure was a few hours, before Ares slowed. His glow had become very faint, and I felt a little pull in my gut as he turned around to face me.

His voice sounded in my head, instead of out loud. "We must rest."

I frowned, but almost immediately schooled my face into indifference. We were being watched by the whole of Olympus. And the God of War did not want the world to know he was tired. The pain of his betrayal in the pits, and the sting of his rejection both times I'd kissed him, made me seriously consider punishing him, forcing him to continue, or admit out loud that he was weak. But he *had* nearly died. And if he wanted to be a jerk he could take more of my power instead of resting, but he wasn't.

"Mortality is a bitch, huh?" I answered him silently. It was too dark to see his reaction, but I made a point of stretching my arms above my head and yawning.

"Armor-boy, I'm freaking starving," I said loudly. "Can we stop and eat?"

. . .

We made a small area against the cave wall as hospitable as we could. We found small boulders to sit on, and Ares scraped some moss off a part of the cave roof that I couldn't reach to pad them. I dug about in dark crevices until I found enough bits of branch and twigs to start a fire.

When we were finally seated around our little campfire, I looked at Ares. "How do we get food? We're not allowed to flash."

"We could ask for help."

"Ask who?"

Ares cocked his head, thinking. "One of my loyal subjects." I raised an eyebrow. "My daughter," he said.

"Woah now, armor-boy. I'm not ready to meet the family," I said, only half joking. It made me feel weird to think of Ares having kids. He looked the right age to have two beaming, gorgeous toddlers, and it was freaky that I knew he had fully-grown ancient demigod offspring roaming the realms of Olympus.

"I believe that you will approve of Hippolyta. She is Queen of the Amazons."

"*The* Amazons? Like where Wonder Woman is from?"

"I do not know who Wonder Woman is, but Hippolyta is a woman and sometimes wondrous."

I barked a laugh, half excited and half shitting myself with nerves. "Does she have a daughter named Diana?"

"No."

"Shame."

"In order to do this, I will need to teach you to communicate with others who wield the power of war."

"Glowing and mind magic, all in one evening. You're spoiling me."

"I thought you wanted to learn? Do you take nothing seriously?"

"I am serious. I'm nervous."

"Stop talking."

"Fine."

My palms were actually sweating a bit in the cool rocky tunnel as Ares leaned forwards, resting his forearms on his knees. "Hold your sword."

I picked *Ischyros* up and lay it flat across my own knees, gripping the hilt. "Think about leading an army. It can be any group of people or creatures you like, but know that you are their leader, their commander. Then invent your opposition. You know what they plan to do, how they are going to do it, and most of all, that you can beat them."

Ares' voice was deep and intense and I closed my eyes. I instantly found myself transported to an expanse of grass and rolling hills as far as the eye could see. And covering every inch of those hills were warriors. Hundreds were on horseback, but more were on foot, and almost all carried crudely fashioned spears, swords, or bows. In the distance was a black line of movement stretching across the horizon. The enemy tribe, marching inexorably toward us. The clothes the soldiers were wearing looked medieval, and I could see no modern technology anywhere in my surroundings. Was I in ancient Britain or Scandinavia?

I looked down at the fictional version of myself. I was wearing a plain purple dress draped with a fur cape, and I had *Ischyros* in one hand, and the shield with the two stallions in the other. And I was mounted on a snow-white horse.

"OK," I breathed aloud to Ares, keeping my eyes closed - reluctant to leave the imaginary scenario that had come so freely to my mind.

"Let the anticipation of the fight build, let your instincts guide your plans. And at the moment the battle begins, hold on to that feeling."

I did as he told me, allowing the rush of the impending battle consume me. I soaked up the adrenaline pouring from those around me, and it was as though their heightened emotions were feeding straight into my veins. The warriors began to sing, low and quiet at first, but my skin tingled as more and more voices joined. Before long the battle chant had become deafening, and the enemy were approaching. They were dressed the same as my own army, but at that moment I didn't care who they were. I was only interested in how to defeat them. I scanned the nearing army, noticing instantly that they had less horses, and more bowmen. My mind worked quickly, calculating how fast my own horsemen could get there, where my soldiers with shields needed to be, and how long it would take to dispatch the archers.

I bellowed commands, and the war song dissipated as the men and women surrounding me obeyed them utterly, my instructions shouted along the rows until everyone knew exactly what they needed to do.

A blissful sense of excitement settled over me, as the sound of the enemy's hooves galloping across the earth increased. It would be only moments until they reached us. Until I could prove the steel of the weapon in my hand, until I could prove myself a true warrior.

"That's it," said Ares, and he sounded like I felt, his tone filled with anticipation. "Now, search for that feeling."

"What?"

"Hold on to that feeling, but come back to the cave. Send out your senses, and search for that feeling around you."

"But I need to be here. I need to fight." *I need to win.*

"It's not real, Bella. It's..." Ares trailed off. "It's your power, manifesting in your imagination. Come back to the cave." Slowly, reluctantly, I opened my eyes. "Good. Don't lose that feeling, search for it. Send your senses out."

Suppressing my disappointment at leaving the vivid imaginary battlefield, I did as he told me, trying to keep the anticipatory elation I was feeling intact. I did what I'd taught myself to do earlier that day, but instead of straining my ears I imagined myself listening for the ringing of steel and the cries of war.

My mouth fell open as white-hot fire leaped up around Ares, the plume on his helmet ablaze. But I knew it wasn't real, it was made of light. My hand reached up automatically, curious.

"You've found me. Look further."

I did as he said, pushing my senses out, and all of a sudden it was like I was on a rollercoaster in the dark. I was zooming through an inky nothingness, and flashing up every now and then around me were similar white flames of light, there and gone before I could slow down to look closer.

"Ares?" I could hear the slight panic in my tone, though I couldn't see anything in the cave any more.

"Slow down. Focus. You want to find Hippolyta."

Lacking any visual to hang on to regarding the Queen of the Amazons, I tried to conjure up a picture of Wonder Woman instead, and almost cried out as my mental rollercoaster jerked back on itself. I whizzed through the darkness, then came crashing to a halt in front of a tower of white fire.

"H-Hippolyta?" I whispered.

A woman stepped from the flames, and my mouth dropped open.

"I permit you entry to my mind only because you are born of my own power. Who are you?"

"Bella. Erm, Enyo. The, erm, Goddess of War," I stammered. God, she was impressive.

She was wearing a brown material tied across her chest and hips with coarse looking rope, with bright red slashes painted across it. Her bare stomach, shoulders and arms were corded with toned muscle, and she twirled a large war-hammer in her left hand. Short blonde hair framed a fierce face, with the brightest blue eyes I'd ever seen.

Her eyebrows lifted, then she gave a small nod. "I had heard of the Trials my father was undertaking, but here in Themiscyra we spurn all outsiders and their nonsense. Why do you seek me?"

"Ares said you might bring us some food. We are in Panic's kingdom, Dasos, in Skotadi, and we are not allowed to flash."

"Why do you not hunt for food?"

"I, erm, don't know," I said, feeling distinctly lame.

Hippolyta scowled. "I shall fulfill my father's wishes," she said, not sounding at all like she wanted to any such thing.

"Thank you," I said, but she had already stepped back into the inferno behind her.

I felt my head jerk as though something was sucking my whole body backwards, and then the dimly lit cave came back into focus around me, Ares staring at me intently from behind his helmet.

"She's..." I started, but before I could finish there was a small flash of red light between us. Something dead, and covered in both scales and feathers, was laid on the floor beside the fire. I cocked my head at it. "I was hoping for a burger."

"She is not happy that I have asked for her help," Ares said wryly.

"No shit. What is that?"

"A rodent."

"It looks like something we could have caught ourselves in the forest."

"I believe that might be the point she was making."

13

BELLA

I couldn't help wondering if we could, in fact, have caught our own food, and Ares had used the idea of asking Hippolyta for help as an excuse to teach me about my war power.

That was what I wanted to believe, at least. We could have tried to contact Zeeva for food, and there was plenty of stuff scurrying about that must have been edible. Asking the Queen of the Amazons for some dinner seemed excessive. He'd refused to teach me anything so many times that it would be hard for him to suddenly backtrack, and I couldn't shift the feeling that something was different since he had nearly drowned. He wasn't using as much of my power either. He could have taken it and spoken to his daughter himself. So why had he got me to do it?

Ares had prepared the animal, and we sat in silence as it turned on a makeshift spit over the little fire.

"Should we sleep here?" I asked him eventually, the quiet too much for me to bear for long.

"I suppose it is as good a place as any, if we must sleep."

"Would carrying on through the night be better? Are dragons any different in the dark?"

He looked up at me, but I couldn't identify his expression. "Take your helmet off," I said softly. He hesitated. "The world has seen your face already."

Slowly, he pulled his helmet off, standing it on the earth beside him with exaggerated care.

"I've seen you quite literally throw that thing at the floor. Why the tenderness now?"

"It's symbolic," he muttered. Firelight flickered across his beautiful face, reflecting in his eyes and softening the hard line of his jaw. He pushed his hair back from his forehead, and I realized I was biting my bottom lip. "Dragons are the same in the dark," he said, and turned the spit with our dinner on it.

"Oh. Do they look like dragons from my world?"

"I have no idea."

"Big scaly things with wings that breath fire?"

"They are large and have scales. They are like winged snakes, with horns."

"Sounds similar," I said.

"They do not breath fire though."

"Oh, good."

"Some are made of fire."

"What?"

"Others from water, but most from muscle. They are very clever. They will try to trick you into doing their bidding, and play games with your mind."

"Right. I can't wait to see which type we get," I breathed.

When the meat was cooked, I realized with some distaste that the only way to eat it was by tearing bits off. Fortunately, my survival instincts were stronger than my gag reflex, and I knew I needed food to stay strong.

"That was gross," I said, after forcing down the last mouthful that I could manage.

"You will offend Hippolyta," Ares said. He seemed to be enjoying his.

"Sorry, Hippolyta," I said, to the cave in general. "She said she hasn't been watching, so she probably won't have heard that," I told Ares.

"No, she would not have been watching. Her tribe are very insular."

"Ares, how do you kill a Keres demon?"

He looked up me. "You can't kill them. They are bound to Hades while they are in his realm. She must be returned."

"Then how do we capture her?"

"If we complete these Trials then we do not need to."

"I'm just curious," I said.

Ares let out a long sigh, fixing his gaze on me. "Bella, besting an ancient death demon is not a feat you can manage alone, and although I understand your need to beat her, you should let go of the idea."

I hadn't expected a God of War to sound so

defeatist. "I have to beat her, to rescue Joshua," I said. But that wasn't entirely true.

I wanted to beat the demon because nobody had ever made me feel so powerless, not because it was the only way to get Joshua back.

"This Joshua," said Ares, dropping his gaze to his knees. "What is he to you?"

"A friend," I said carefully. "He helped me when I was very frustrated and unhappy."

"Why were you unhappy?"

"I already told you, I knew I didn't belong. I had too much energy for the world I was in. I was drawn to extremes, things that didn't fit with what I actually wanted in my heart."

"I don't understand." He looked up at me again, his expression serious.

I sighed. "In my heart, I want justice, fairness, kindness. Love. But the need to feel alive, to challenge everything, to find and push boundaries, drove me to places that were filled with the opposite of kindness and love. And my confrontational urges meant that I caused chaos in those places. Many times, I was close to destroying things, even people. It made me very unhappy, but I didn't know why or how to fix it. Therapy with Joshua helped me understand that there were two sides to my soul, one constantly angry and one constantly seeking joy. He helped me find ways to expel the anger safely."

"I am sorry."

I blinked in surprise. "That's not a word I've heard

you use, even when you should have. Why are you sorry?"

A darkness filled his eyes as he stared at me across the campfire. "I did not realize this man was so important to you."

I frowned. Was he jealous? "He's my only friend." I put weight on the world friend, though I wasn't sure why. Ares and I were not a thing. Did it matter if I had a crush on my shrink?

Ares lifted his hand to his jaw, drawing his fingers across his stubble thoughtfully. An intense longing to replace his fingers with mine rose up in me, and I coughed awkwardly.

"We will win the Trials and return him to you. I do not feel like sleeping. We should continue." He stood up abruptly, picking up his helmet. I shook my head. When Ares decided the conversation was over, it was over.

"What if *I* feel like sleeping?" He narrowed his eyes at me, then pulled his helmet on. "Fine. Whatever." I stood, kicking dust over the fire, annoyed. "Why is everything always your way?"

"Because you know nothing about this world." He began to glow faintly as the fire went out, and I pictured the gleaming sails in my mind, satisfied when my own skin began to glow too.

"Tell me more about it then."

"Later."

"You know, you may have been created just to make me roll my eyes," I told him, as he set off through the cave.

We hadn't been moving long when I became aware of the scuttling sound I'd first heard when we entered the tunnel.

"What's that noise?" I asked in a loud whisper.

"It could be many things."

"Real helpful. Glad I asked."

I gripped my sword tighter, feeling it heat in my palm. It had been too long since something had tried to kill us. As if on cue with my thoughts, a sudden gust of air whooshed down the tunnel over us, bringing with it a rank smell of rotten meat. Ares stopped, then turned to me.

"Do you wish to test your power?"

"Yes," I nodded vigorously.

"The feeling of war that you used earlier to find Hippolyta can be used in battle. It will trigger what you experienced with the hundred-hander. Your movements will speed up, and it will feel as though your opponent will slow down. You will be able to anticipate their reactions and decisions with ease."

"OK." Ares nodded, then turned and resumed his march, his steps more cautious than before. "Why are you telling me things?" I asked, following him equally as warily.

"You will need the knowledge to kill whatever we are about to face."

"I thought you were planning to take care of everything yourself?"

"My plans have changed."

"Why?"

"This is not the place to discuss such things."

I made an exasperated noise, but said nothing else. I had suspected earlier that Ares was finding excuses to teach me how to use my power, and something had definitely changed. If he didn't want to tell me in public what was going on then I'd have to wait until we'd dealt with this dragon and we were alone.

Gods, I wanted to be alone with him.

"Stop," Ares hissed suddenly. I did, pushing out my senses as I halted. The rancid smell strengthened first, then the gold glow coming from the two of us brightened as my eyesight improved, lighting areas of the cave walls previously too dark to see. There was a slight film covering them, I realized. It was pale and fine and reminded me of...

"A spider's web," I whispered, a trickle of dread spreading through my gut. "Ares, please tell me there are no giant spiders in your realm."

"What is a spider?" he murmured, his head tipped back as he scanned the ceiling.

"Round body, too many fucking legs," I hissed, following suit. My blood froze in my veins as something as big as a car scuttled across the rocky ceiling over our heads and into the shadows faster than I could make out, even with my super senses.

"It's an arachnida," Ares said, and for some reason he sounded slightly relieved. "You can beat it."

"*I* can beat it? You mean we? We can beat it?"

"No. This time you fight alone."

"Why?"

"To prove that you can." His voice sounded in my head, not aloud, and I couldn't help looking away from where I was frantically searching the shadows for a car-sized spider, and fixing my eyes on him. *"Show the world what I denied you of in Erimos."*

He wasn't looking at me, and nobody watching would have any idea that he was speaking to me at all. He was giving me this fight to let me show off to Olympus. This was his version of an apology, I realized.

Under any normal circumstance I would have been excited. Touched, even, by his thoughtfulness. But why the fuck did it have to be when we were fighting a fucking giant spider?

I opened my mouth to say as much, but my pride barreled through my fear before I could speak. Was I really about to throw away an opportunity to show the world what I was made of? I never backed down from a challenge. I mean, I'd never been challenged by a giant spider before, but still. This was a chance to show Aphrodite that I wasn't as little as she believed I was. Plus, it was a chance to test my growing power, with Ares to back me up for a change, instead of him trying to take it away.

I couldn't turn this down.

"Come at me, spider-scum," I hissed, raising *Ischyros*.

14

BELLA

Whatever an arachnida was, it wasn't an actual spider, I told myself as we moved further into the darkness, me now leading the way. It was just another Greek monster. We'd got past a load of them already. This would be no different.

"Do they bite?"

"No, they sting."

"Everything here stings," I murmured.

"Now you mention it, yes."

My super-sense hearing had lost the scuttling sound, which made me extremely wary. The thing was staying still. I was raking my honed eyesight over the cave walls and ceiling, and therefore totally missed the creature shooting out of the blackness directly in front of me until it was almost too late.

I slashed *Ischyros* down in front of me in a wide arc just in time, and the huge black thing darted backwards and made an awful screeching sound.

It really was as big as a car, and it really was basically a giant spider. It had plated scales instead of fur, and a massive stinger on its ass, but it was definitely a spider. Eight enormous legs held up its disgusting body, and they clicked as the thing moved backwards and forwards, its network of honeycomb-shaped eyes flashing as they caught the gold of my glowing light.

I took a breath as I dropped into a crouch instinctively. I didn't like spiders. In fact, there weren't many creepy crawlies I liked less.

I needed this thing to not even register as a spider in my mind; it was a monster. Spiders were gross because they crawled all over you, fast and tickly and freaky. This creature was something else entirely, that belonged to Olympus, totally new and different. And it reeked.

Remembering what Ares had told me before, I tried to recall that feeling on the battle field as the arachnida and I circled each other. I could make out Ares' faint glow in my broad peripheral vision, far behind me but moving with us. Without warning, the arachnida's ass swerved under its body and a jet of something shot out of it toward me. I leaped to the side and swiped with my sword, immediately regretting it when whatever it was stuck to the end of my blade. I scowled as I realized what it was. Web. The thing was trying to cover me in sticky ass cobwebs.

The clicking of the spider's legs tripled in speed and then it was coming for me again. Pulling on the hot well of power inside me, I raised my sword and threw myself forward, trying to get underneath its body.

"Use the power of war." Ares' voice sounded in my head and as I slid under the creature I groped for the battlefield feeling again.

Just as I got underneath the spider's big body the stinger moved again, curling underneath itself only feet from me. The version of me in the purple dress, mounted on the white steed and holding that epic shield slammed into my mind, and I was vaguely aware of the glow I was giving off bursting into bright life. The web firing from the stinger bounced harmlessly off my invisible barrier, and with a roar, I willed *Ischyros* to grow.

It did, and fast. As the blade made contact with the monster's underbelly it was already twice the size it had been. I filled the muscles of my arms with power as the blade got heavier, feeling my whole body swell in reaction, then rolled as I pulled the blade through the arachnida's body. Its legs gave out immediately and I jumped to my feet as its body followed, collapsing onto the cave floor.

I'd won.

"Good," said Ares, aloud.

I looked between my blade and him. The sword was massive, almost as tall as me in fact. I concentrated a moment, and couldn't help smiling as *Ischyros* began to shrink down. "This is cool as fuck," I said.

Ares stepped around the dead arachnida and I got a glimpse of his eyes. Fire was dancing in them. Swirling energy from the too-short fight redirected itself instantly to the increasingly desperate area between my thighs.

"Your weapon should be warm, not cool."

I blinked at him, then realized what he meant. "The word cool means good in my world."

"That makes no sense."

"No, probably not." I shrugged. "I want to fight more stuff." *Or fuck you until you make me scream.* The alternative flashed unexpectedly into my head, and I felt my cheeks get hot. Fighting and fucking. I knew lots of fighters from the underground rings who connected the two, but I'd never been one of them. Until now, apparently.

"We should keep moving," Ares said.

We walked through the tunnel for what felt like an age, adrenaline and anticipation keeping my golden glow bright and hot. We passed the bodies of many dead things, presumably killed by the arachnida, but nothing living or dangerous. Eventually the tunnel began to narrow, and with some relief I saw a dim patch of daylight in the distance.

"Use your shield when we exit," grunted Ares.

"Yes, sir," I said, giving his armor-clad back a salute. I saw him shake his head a little.

When we emerged from the stinking cave tunnel it wasn't into forest as I had expected, but into a colossal stone ruin. The dusty expanse of broken rock cracked as our booted feet moved over it, the noise loud in the silence. I slowly stepped in a circle, surveying the wrecked structure.

It had once been a fighting pit, I was sure. But the stepped seats that must have lined one side had crumbled to nothing, revealing the maze of rooms beneath. The benches had remained a little intact on the other side, but I wouldn't have risked testing my weight on them. Opposite the tunnel mouth we'd just come from, the circular walls of the pit had disintegrated completely, and the oppressive forest had started to make progress in swallowing the pit, tree roots spreading across what would have been the pit floor like gnarled fingers reaching for us.

I sent out my senses, wary of the oxys, but I couldn't hear any buzzing. I did hear something else though. Something that sounded like heavy breathing. The hairs stood up on my skin as a feeling I didn't recognize crawled over my body. It was as though I'd been doused in cold water, whilst an utterly certain knowledge that something awful was about to happen lodged in my mind.

"Ares? You feel that?" I whispered.

"I think we have found our dragon."

15

ARES

My desire for the woman raising her sword beside me was becoming so intense I was no longer sure I could manage it. And now I was certain it wasn't just physical. The thought of her coming to any harm caused a blind rage to stir inside me, and fear to coil through my gut. I was Ares, God of War. I was supposed to fear nothing.

I had to teach her to use her power. I had to make her stronger. Seeing her fight and use the power of war was addictive, her glow like a drug I couldn't get enough of. Her fierce spirit gleamed like no aura I had ever seen in a god before.

I needed more.

The sound of stone cracking and wood creaking snapped my attention to where the lethal forest was spilling into the ruined pit. The wood of the trees was moving, the gnarled roots lifting. With lethal grace, a creature morphed into being before us, from where it had been camouflaged so perfectly.

The dragon was made from wood, its body long and sinewy like a snake's as it slithered into the space on the floor of the pit. Its reptilian head had a mane of sharp horns, and its enormous jaws were lined with ferocious teeth, bared bright at us. Vividly green eyes gleamed in the sides of its swaying head, and it snapped its wings out taut as it came to a stop. They too were born of the forest, the arch and boning of the wings made from thick branches, the matter filling the gaps like sheer leaves.

It was a magnificent looking beast.

"Oh my god, it's stunning," I heard Bella mutter, her voice awed.

"You're too kind," the dragon said. Bella made a small squeak. "You are here to seek me?"

"May we know your name?" I asked the beast loudly.

"Of course, if you are willing to part with yours."

Fierce intelligence flashed in the dragon's eyes. This would not be easy. All dragons were ancient and wise, and it was clear this one was no exception. "I am Ares, God of War, and this is Enyo, Goddess of War." Nerves skittered through me on saying Bella's real name. Depending on the age of this particular beast, he may know more about Bella than I wanted her to know. But if he was who I suspected he was, then it would do no good to lie to him.

The dragon swayed his head from side to side as he surveyed us. He was massive, his coiled body filling half the ruined pit. His tree-bark like scales made up rings that spiraled around his entire length, each individual scale as large as my chest.

"I am Dentro."

My stomach clenched at his words, my worst suspicions confirmed. "I have heard of you," I said. "You are ancient indeed."

"Far more ancient than you, little Olympian."

Anger surged through me, and I reached automatically for Bella's power. I felt no resistance from her. "The *little Olympians* rule the world, Dentro," I said loudly. The creature's lips curled back in an approximation of a smile, and he chuckled.

"Your father and his two brothers rule the world. You can't even hold onto your own power, it seems, let alone rule."

"At least I'm not hiding in a forest," I snarled. It didn't matter how old he was, I would not allow this animal to mock me.

"You are as bound to your situation as I am, little god."

"I am bound to nothing."

"Oh, but you are, Ares. You are bound by everyone stronger than you. You are bound by your own pride. You are bound by your own fear." He hissed the last word and rage erupted through me.

"I fear nothing!" I roared. Bella's power, my power, called to me as the rage spilled over, and she let me take it. I grew fast, tearing toward Dentro.

I heard a roar behind me, and in a flash Bella was running beside me, her face fierce and her skin glowing as gold as my armor. Her power was blinding, all consuming, and she drowned everything else out completely. This was war, and together we would win.

16

BELLA

The mix of fear and excitement I felt as we charged toward the dragon was intoxicating.

Dentro was the most incredible thing I had ever seen, and no amount of my imagination could have conjured him up. His snake-like body was made up of one long spiral of rich brown tree-bark which moved seamlessly as he reared back. Tufts of deep green moss were lodged between the rows of scales and I didn't know if it was growing from his body or had just been gathered up as he slithered through the forest. His wings spread wide behind him and my heightened senses brought the green substance between the bark-bones to life, veined like leaves and vivid in color. The horns around his head appeared to be growing, and large spikes that looked like murderous blades of grass were spreading between them.

He was nature personified, and at its most lethal.

"What do you seek?" His voice rang through the

derelict pit, though his mouth didn't move with the words. Ares and I split, he running to the left and I to the right. I had a plan, and somehow I knew that Ares was thinking the same thing. The invisible cord connecting us was humming with life, power flowing between us.

When we didn't answer him, Dentro spoke again. "You will answer me."

The ground beneath us shook so hard I stumbled. Slamming down onto one knee, I only just managed to hang on to *Ischyros* and as I started to push myself to my feet the huge wooden body of the dragon whipped toward me. I tried to move, the war-sight kicking in instinctively and the world slowing around me. But it wasn't slow enough. Dentro's enormous tail coiled around my middle before I could fully stand, and I beat at it frantically with my sword. I tried to raise my shield to force him off me, but he squeezed tighter, the shield useless. The coarse wood of his scales scratched at my skin painfully, and suddenly I was lifted off my feet. With a lurching sensation I was swung around, coming to a stop directly in front of the dragon's gaping maw.

"Now, tell me, Enyo. What do you seek?"

"Dentro!" I could hear Ares bellowing somewhere below me. The tail that was wrapped around me was too huge to see past, and I only had my sword arm free. I smashed my weapon repeatedly against the wooden scales, but I knew it was doing no harm to the awesome beast.

"As you're new to this world, I'm going to let you in on a little secret." The dragon's voice was deep and seductive as he lifted me to look directly into one of his bright green eyes. "I'm even older than some of the Titans. You can't do any damage with that little blade of yours. Now, tell me what you seek."

"Scales," I barked, refusing to stop trying, pouring my power into the blows.

"*My* scales?" The dragon sounded amused.

"Yes."

"What in Olympus do you want my scales for?"

"We were challenged to get them by the king of this realm, Panic."

Something dark flashed in Dentro's eyes, and I stopped beating him with my sword for long enough to get my breath back. "That swine thinks he can use me as a toy in his games, does he? Hmmmm. Why did you accept his challenge?"

"To capture an escaped hell-demon and rescue my friend."

"Interesting. Is this true?"

He swung me violently to the side and moved his head fast, bringing it almost to the ground in front of Ares. The god looked furious.

"Yes! Release her!" He was easily ten feet tall, and his sword was as big as he was.

"No. But, as you are here on a genuinely noble cause, I will offer you an opportunity. How many scales of mine do you require?"

"Three," I said, biting back a curse as my thrashing scratched up more of the skin on my arms and shoulders.

"I will give you the scales, if you get something for me in return."

"We are not puppets!" roared Ares.

The dragon laughed, and the ground shook again, the ruins around us cracking and crumbling loudly. "Then I shall kill you both."

"You can't kill us, we're immortal," I said, resuming my battering with *Ischyros* with renewed vigor, ignoring the lacerations covering my skin.

"No, you're not. Not as long as you're sharing this strange power of yours."

My heart skipped a beat. "What?"

"I am ancient. I can see the cord between you. And only one of you can be a true god - which will leave the other as good as human. For one to be immortal, the other must die."

A trickle of dread slid down my spine. I *knew* he was speaking the truth. We'd as much as proved his words when we had almost drowned. Ares had to give up the power for me to breathe underwater.

But I had hoped that as I became stronger I would have enough power for both of us to be strong. For both of us to be immortal. I found Ares' eyes, my attacks with *Ischyros* momentarily forgotten.

Ares knew the words were true too. I could see it in his eyes. Perhaps he had already known.

"What do you want us to do?" Ares asked, his voice strong and proud, with no hint of the turmoil my brain was currently going through. We were back to only one of us being able to be strong, just as it had been when he'd first found me and wanted to kill me for my power.

But things were different now. He was different now. Wasn't he?

"Is Panic watching us?"

"The world is watching us."

Dentro straightened, lifting me high with him, then bent his serpentine neck in a mock bow. "Hello, Olympus," he said, and bared his terrifying teeth. "I'm afraid this conversation must be private."

The sounds of branches cracking suddenly filled the air, and my mouth fell open as forest flowed into being around us, cocooning us in an enormous leafy bubble.

"What I am about to tell you is forbidden knowledge. But for too long I have spent my life a slave to another. I am willing to break my dragon's oath, in the hope that you are noble enough to honor me." Dentro lowered himself back to the ground, taking me with him, and to my surprise setting me back on the stone. His tail slowly uncoiled, and a wave of relief washed through me. Ares stepped closer and then stopped, almost as if he hadn't meant to.

"Heal your wounds," he snarled. I looked down at the smears of blood trickling from the many shallow cuts from the bark, but focused instead on Dentro.

"Who are you a slave to? Panic?" I asked the dragon.

His huge green eyes filled with anger. "When the Titans created beings as powerful as dragons, they needed to ensure we could be controlled. Panic has something of mine that allows him to keep me here, in his forest, to scare people and make himself look more

powerful. His lethal pet. I can't leave here as long as he
has it. I am trapped. A prisoner."

"What does he have?"

Dentro swooped his head lower, and I held out my
weapon defensively as his massive mouth moved close
to us. But as he opened his jaws, he spoke. "He stole my
tooth." I realized he was showing us the gap in the row
of shiny, razor sharp teeth, and I dropped my
sword arm.

"Dragons can be controlled by whomever has their
teeth?" For the first time since I'd met him, Ares
sounded surprised.

"Yes. Teeth, and somewhat more unpleasantly, eyes.
If you steal those from a dragon, you can impose your
will on them enough to imprison them."

"Can he force you to do things you don't want
to do?"

"Not unless he has all my teeth, no. I am too strong.
You must swear never to share this knowledge. My
kind's persecution and imprisonment depends on it."

"I swear," I said without hesitation. We both looked
at Ares when he said nothing.

"I am bound to share knowledge like this with my
father," he said slowly.

Dentro snorted. "Zeus is fully aware of this. How do
you think he has kept the most powerful dragon in the
world, Ladon, under his control for so long?"

Ares was still a moment, then nodded. "Fine. I
swear it."

"Good. Steal my tooth back from Panic and return it
to me. Free me from this dead place."

I felt my eyebrows raise. "*Steal* it from him? How?"

"I do not know. But as you two are the most powerful beings I have encountered in centuries, you are my best, and likely only, hope."

I didn't know if it was the deep, earnest tone to the dragon's voice, or if it was the fierce intelligence in his huge eyes, but I trusted him. I wanted to help him. Nobody should be held captive against their will. The dark days I had spent in prison flashed through my mind, and I looked to Ares. The god's voice sounded in my head.

"He could be trying to trick us. Dragons are famous for playing mind games."

"I like him," I answered mentally. *"I think we should do it."*

"Liking him has nothing to do with it."

"Yes it does."

Before Ares could say anything else, I spoke aloud. "We'll do it." Excitement danced in Dentro's eyes and his tail swished against the leaf bubble.

"You will earn my eternal gratitude if you succeed."

Ares growled beside me. I'd definitely pissed him off answering for both of us. But I didn't care. This was the right thing to do, I knew it was.

"How are we supposed to get your tooth back from here?" he ground out. "I assume if it was hidden in the forest you would have found it yourself by now."

"I believe Panic has a trophy room in his castle. It is my guess that my tooth will be there."

"We can't leave this forest without your scales."

Dentro paused, then fixed his eyes on me. "I will

allow you to take the scales now. But you must promise to return with my tooth as soon as you can."

"Why would you trust us?" I asked, cocking my head.

Dentro stared at me, and I could feel his magic. Not working against me, messing with my mind or forcing me to feel anything fake, but more like an aura, or a glimpse of his soul. He *was* the personification of nature, wild and free and fierce and bright and strong. And he was trapped in a dark, lifeless forest, his essence fading with his hope. "I have no choice but to trust you," he said quietly.

I felt a kinship with this incredible, beautiful creature; I understood him, I felt his pain. I would help free him, whatever it took. I had to. I reached my hand up instinctively, and his massive tail flicked around, slowing to a stop an inch from my fingers.

"We'll get your tooth," I said.

"Thank you." His rough tail met my hand, and I felt a burst of bright hope spread through me, then a warm tingle in my skin as the cuts covering me instantly healed.

Somehow, I had just befriended an ancient, all-powerful dragon.

I freaking loved Olympus.

17

BELLA

When Dentro dissolved the leaf bubble hiding us from the rest of Olympus, I was clutching the three scales that the dragon had allowed me to gently prise from his tail. With one last pointed look, the magnificent creature melted back into the forest that was spilling into the derelict fighting pit, and I felt a pang of something as I watched him go. Excitement, or anticipation, or maybe both. I could feel Ares' anger with me rolling off him in waves, and I had absolutely zero idea how we would actually get our hands on Dentro's stolen tooth, but I knew I'd done the right thing. Whatever it was I had felt from the dragon was more than just awe or respect, and he deserved to be free.

It wouldn't be easy though. The whole of Olympus would have seen us disappear into the dragon's magic leaf bubble, and it would be obvious that we had not fought and defeated the creature. I took a deep breath, wishing I could talk to Ares in private, so that we could work out our story before we had to face the Lords.

"What do we tell Panic?" I asked him in my head, trying to keep my face impassive.

"This is your mess. You work it out," he growled back. I locked eyes with him, and my stomach clenched as I saw how dark his were.

"Fine," I said, tightening my arms around the scales, then lifting them higher. "We have your scales, Panic!" I bellowed, holding up the massive sections of heavy tree bark.

"So I see." The Lord's voice echoed through the crumbling pit. "Congratulations. I'll give you the opportunity to tell us all how you managed to coax them out of the beast at a ball in your honor this evening. Put the scales on the ground."

I bent down, doing as he asked. The second they were out of my grip, everything flashed white and we were no longer in Skotadi.

I let out a long breath as I looked around at the tiny wooden cabin with the ugly couches.

"If the ball Panic is throwing is at his castle, then that's the perfect opportunity to find the tooth!" I said excitedly, turning to Ares. I almost took a step back as he pulled his helmet off, his expression was so fierce.

"You are reckless and foolish and selfish!"

"What?"

"We are not here to do favors for dragons stupid

enough to get themselves trapped! We are supposed to be getting my power back!"

Indignation rolled through me as I took a step closer to the fuming god. "No, we're supposed to be stopping the Keres demon and saving the Guardians. Your Trident of power was an added bonus, if I remember correctly. And besides, it's the right thing to do."

"Whatever the point of our quest, it has nothing to do with damn dragons."

"How the hell else were we going to win that Trial? Dentro could have killed me with one squeeze! He was too strong for us to defeat, and you know it. So did Panic, that's why he sent us there."

Ares stamped his foot and flames burst to life in his eyes as I felt a pull in my gut. I stepped closer to him, as though the pull was physical. "We could have defeated him! We could defeat any foe!"

"Look, Mr Stampy, he nearly fucking killed me. One squeeze, and I was a goner. Panic set us an impossible task, and we won. Take the damn victory." A solitary drum beat loud in the distance. Ares closed the gap between us.

"He would not have killed you. You are immortal." His voice was just as angry, but no longer loud. Fire leaped in his eyes.

"Then he would have killed you instead. Only one of us can be immortal, remember?" I answered, my voice needlessly breathless. My heart was beginning to pound in my chest. He was beautiful. So damned beautiful.

"We need to finish the next Trial, and get your friend and my power back. We do not have time to help the dragon."

His words were like ice water over the heat in my core. "What? No, we get Dentro's tooth. Now, tonight, at this ball."

"Bella, we are not risking the Lords' wrath before these Trials are over." Fury swept through me like a freight train, and I had taken three steps back from him before I'd even realized I'd moved.

"I gave Dentro my word, dammit, and I am not letting him down. *Not risking the Lords' wrath?* Do you fear them?"

I knew the question would anger him, and I was right. His whole body swelled with rage, but when he tugged on my power, I slammed my shields down. His glow dimmed, and his face darkened further.

"It is not the Lords I fear," he hissed, and even without any power he was menacing as hell.

"Then why aren't you celebrating this victory? We won the damn Trial! Why aren't you reveling in the opportunity to take something from that asshole that he values, to return an almighty creature back to full power, to do some fucking good for once!"

"Because we do not know the cost!" he roared back at me.

"Who cares? You're a fucking god, what can they take from you? You've already lost your power, and the Lords can't kill you - the Olympians wouldn't allow it! What cost could be too high?"

"You!"

I blinked at his shouted word, the fire in his irises burning fierce with emotion. "Me?"

"You." His voice was ragged, like the word had been torn forcibly from his throat. My pulse was racing now, a hope I had never known swamping my chest, making my own throat tighten.

"Ares... What do you want?" I half whispered the question, desperate to hear one word in answer. More than anything in the world, I wanted him to say *you*. I wanted him to say he feared losing me. That whatever it was between us was more than physical, that it wasn't just my imagination running rampant. His lips parted and my breath caught. *Say you want me as much as I want you.*

"Knock knock?" I almost jumped out of my skin as Eris' voice rang loudly through the room, then she appeared with an overly bright flash. Disappointment crashed through me, and I heard Ares let out a hiss of anger as I focused on the Goddess of Chaos. Her eyes went wide and she clasped her hands to her lips in mock embarrassment.

"Oh my, oh my, I've interrupted something! I'm so sorry, sweeties." Her smile reached all the way to her eyes, and I took a heaving breath as my pulse continued its gallop. Eris' curly hair was piled even higher on her head than usual, and she was wearing a long, tight dress that glittered with black sequins and barely contained her huge chest.

"You're dressed nice," I said, scrabbling for something normal and not-awkward to say.

"Thanks, sweetie. I'm here to help you do the same.

All the gods are coming to the ball, and whilst I'm a fan of this look, I thought you might do a bit better this time."

"Er, thanks."

"I thought you were in hiding," growled Ares.

"I was. Now I'm not."

Unable to stand still, I walked to the bed, dropping my sword onto the comforter, and starting to absently pull bits of forest out of my hair. Waves of emotion were rolling through me, desire and anger balling up into something difficult to contain. It made me furious that Ares didn't want to help Dentro, but was the reason truly that he feared for me? Nobody had feared for my safety in my whole life. Joshua had cared about me, but actually feared for me? I didn't think so.

Dragging my thoughts into line, I tried to work out what to do and say next.

Whatever Ares' motivations were for not wanting to help the dragon, I was getting that tooth. That much I knew for sure. And so long as Eris was here, I was pretty sure she could help.

"Do you know where this ball is going to be?" I asked her, crossing my fingers she was going to say Panic's castle.

"Here in Dasos I believe; Terror's kingdom is not suited to balls."

I suppressed a desire to ask more about Terror's kingdom, and nodded. "Good. I hope it's not in that drafty, crumbling place we were in before when he announced the Trial."

"I doubt it, Panic will want to show off to the gods."

Excellent.

There was a flash of teal, and Zeeva appeared on the bed before me. My heart did a small flutter at the surprise, and my hands tensed into fists.

"I wish everyone would stop doing that," I snarled. Zeeva flicked her tail when she looked at Eris, then focused her almond eyes on me.

"What deal did you make with the dragon?" she asked bluntly, her voice crystal clear in my head.

"It's nice to see you safe and sound too," I said, rolling my eyes.

"You went into the creature's leaf shield his captive, and came out a victor. You offered it something in return for those scales. What was it?"

"That's what I want to know too," smiled Eris, and sat down gracefully on the peach couch.

"Stop listening in!"

"I can't help it."

"Bella agreed to steal something valuable from Panic's castle for the dragon." I looked at Ares in surprise as he spoke. He didn't sound angry any more. In fact, he sounded proud. "And we're going to do it tonight, at the ball, with help from both of you."

My mouth fell open as I stared at the warrior god. His eyes flicked to mine as Eris spoke.

"I do love a bit of theft," she said.

"I know, sister. Your help will be invaluable to us."

"And what do I get in return, little brother?"

"What do you want?"

"Let me think about it," she purred.

"Fine. Don't take too long." Ares turned to Zeeva. "Cat?"

"Theft is not in my remit," she said haughtily.

"But helping Bella is. And we only won that Trial because she made this deal." His eyes locked on mine as he said the words. Was that another Ares-style apology? He *had* just admitted out loud that we would have lost to Dentro.

"I will do what I can to help, if it does not compromise my morals," sighed Zeeva.

"Thank you," I told her. *"You've changed your tune."* I projected the words to Ares silently.

"My anger was misplaced. I do not like meeting beings stronger than I," he answered in my head.

"Me neither."

"I will endeavor to enjoy upsetting Panic by stealing from him. You were right. This will be a victory, of sorts."

"Say that again."

"Say what?"

"The bit about me being right."

18

BELLA

"OK. This is how it needs to go."

We all sat on the squishy couches, listening to Eris.

"Zeeva. If you don't want to be involved in any actual stealing, then we could use you now. All three of us would be noticed by Panic if we entered his castle, as we share his power. But you should be able to get in undetected. Go now, and find out where he keeps his trophies and valuables."

After a small pause, the cat stood and stretched. *"I suppose that is manageable,"* she said, then vanished in a puff of teal.

"You two," said Eris, a smile pulling at her lips as she looked between Ares and me. "You two will need a credible reason to disappear from the party." Her eyes shone with mischief. "Which means making a show of wanting to be alone together. Based on that kiss the whole of Olympus saw, I'm assuming that won't be too difficult for either of you?"

I felt myself blush, and avoided looking at Ares.

"I'll take that as a no," she laughed. "I'll do my best to distract Panic, and trust me, I can come up with some very distracting scenarios, but then it'll be up to you to steal your prize. Do you care if you are caught?"

Ares' shoulders straightened. "Panic can't do a thing about it, I am his ruler."

"We care about getting the prize safely away from the castle," I interrupted. "The idea is to do that without drawing any attention to what we are doing." I looked pointedly at Ares. We'd sworn to keep what we had learned a secret, and that meant we had to avoid questions being asked publicly.

"OK. It's likely you won't be able to flash if you're in a vault or secure place. So you may have to sneak your way out of there." Eris looked at me.

I nodded. "OK."

"We should start getting you ready." Eris stood abruptly, and swirled her hand around until a ball of fabric appeared in it, growing as she swirled more. It was the same purple as the dress that the version of me in my vision of war had on.

"What do I need to do?" I asked her.

Her lips puckered as she looked me up and down. "Keep getting all that forest-shit out of your hair, then shower."

When I entered the main room of the cabin wrapped only in a towel after showering, I saw Zeeva curled up on the bed. "How did it go?" I asked her, excited to find out what she had learned.

"Panic's trophy room is at the top of the third smallest tower in the castle, on the north-east side. The staircase is rigged so that one false step will send you into a pit below full of oxys. The door at the top can only be entered by someone who possesses the power of Panic. The trophies within are encased in unbreakable glass."

I could feel my face falling as she spoke, each sentence sounding worse than the last.

"It's nothing we can't handle," said Ares, his voice brimming with confidence. I looked to him in surprise. I had expected him to go all *I-told-you-so* on my ass, not sound excited. He wasn't wearing his armor, and my gaze snagged on the open collar of his shirt. "We do possess the power of Panic, it feeds into the power of war."

"What about the staircase?"

"There will be a way through. We will have to outsmart it." His eyes gleamed with excitement, and as I looked into them I felt my stomach flutter.

"And the unbreakable glass?"

"There is nothing the God of War can't break. Trust me." The look on his face sent thrills running through me. I knew, fundamentally, that a man telling me there was nothing he couldn't break shouldn't turn me on. But hell, the truth was that had I been wearing panties, they might have melted off, such was the heat he fired within me. His eyes raked over my bare shoulders, before coming back to my face, and I felt my tongue dart out to wet my lips. I hadn't seen him like this except after the Hydra fight, and his energy was infectious. A buzz of anticipation rolled off him, and I absorbed it greedily.

"Ares, you need to leave. I need to dress Bella. And the way you two are looking at each other, I do not want to be here when she drops that towel. You're my brother. Gross."

I felt my cheeks flush as Ares moved toward the door. "Fine. I will be no longer than thirty minutes."

I heard the door slam as he left, and I reached for him with my mind, unable to help myself. *"I would have dropped the towel for you. If we had been alone."*

I didn't expect him to reply, and I almost let out a moan when his husky voice filled my head a second later. *"I would have ripped it from you with my teeth."*

The whole time Eris was tightening bits of fabric around my body, fluffing skirts and doing something almost-but-not-quite painful to my hair, all I could think about was Ares. Naked. Desire was spilling over every useful or rational thought I had about the heist we were about to try and pull off, and I was unable to concentrate on anything other than the memory of the two kisses we had shared.

I wanted to keep talking to him in my mind, but his answer had been so hungry, so unexpected and so sexy that instead I just hung on to it, replaying the growl of need I had heard in his tone that mirrored my own intensity.

"I don't know why Ares doesn't just tell Panic to give him whatever it is. He is his ruler, after all." Zeeva sounded bored, but I was sure I could hear an undercurrent to her tone.

"Nobody in this realm is honest, least of all those in charge," said Eris. "He would just lie and say he doesn't have it, and Ares is not currently strong enough to challenge him."

"What if I gave him my strength?" I asked.

"No. You are probably level in power with the Lords right now. At his full power Ares would be many times stronger."

"Oh. Are the Lords immortal?"

"No. Not as such. Their hosts can be killed, but the power they embody returns to Ares, until he bestows it on someone new."

My stomach skittered uneasily. "Is that what would happen to my power if I die?"

"Yes."

Which was why Ares had originally planned to kill me, I thought, with an awkward stomach twist. "Why didn't Ares try to kill them and get their power when his was stolen?"

"You'd have to ask him that. But he was the one who chose to bestow Pain, Panic and Terror on other souls in the first place. They are not powers he is interested in possessing. Besides, until you showed up he was too weak to fight them and win anyway."

I glanced at Eris over my shoulder, where she was

tightening a choker necklace around my throat. "Did Ares bestow my power on me, like the Lords?"

"Bella, I honestly have no idea where you have come from. I thought I did for a while, but I was wrong."

Zeeva gave a loud yawn, and we both looked at her. *"My mistress knows."*

Excitement flashed through me, making my skin feel tight all of a sudden. "Tell me!"

"I can't. She says you must find out for yourself."

Frustration made my hands fist, and I ground my teeth. "Why mention it then?" I spat. "Just to piss me off?"

"Oh, there is plenty to be gleaned from what your cat has just said," grinned Eris. "If Hera knows where you came from, then we can safely assume she knows where you'll end up. Or at least who you'll end up with."

"What?"

"Hera is the goddess of marriage. And when gods marry, they are bonded. For life. Physically and mentally."

I felt my chest constricting at Eris' words, suddenly distinctly aware of the cord I could always feel connecting me to Ares. But that was our shared power, nothing more. Wasn't it? "What are you saying?"

"Just that Hera knows when two gods are meant to be together," Eris shrugged. Her eyes were sparkling with amusement.

"Gods can't just go around bonding people without their permission!" I spluttered.

"No, of course they can't," said Zeeva calmly. *"My mistress only ever bonds deities who are deeply in love."*

Relief swept through me. It was one thing to wrangle my head into understanding my desire for the ridiculously gorgeous warrior god. That sort of made sense. He was hot as hell, strong, fierce, proud.

It was quite another thing to contend with the thought of being in love with him. He had the emotional capacity of a teenage boy, and didn't seem to have much interest in basic human rights. Not exactly husband material.

"Will Hera be at the ball tonight?" I asked Zeeva hopefully.

"No."

"What's wrong with her? She's not been seen since Zeus fled," said Eris. Her tone was casual, but I could tell she was burning with curiosity. I had to admit to being pretty curious myself.

"She is unwell."

"Olympians gods do not get unwell," said Eris, her eyebrows raised and her hands on her hips.

Zeeva said nothing, just rested her head on her neat little paws. It was exactly the sort of position I would have cooed over when I thought she was just my grumpy pet cat.

"Erm, Zeeva, when you lived in my apartment, did you like being petted?" I asked hesitantly.

After a long pause, the cat answered. *"It wasn't so bad, I suppose."*

19

ARES

Bella was stunning. So stunning that I almost felt inadequate in my armor beside her. Eris had fashioned her hair with some sort of delicate gold headdress, which caged in her pale curls. Tiny glittering swords hung from the sweeping metal curves, catching the light that came from her glowing skin. Her dress was fit for a goddess too. It was purple, and like the last one it was tight around her curvaceous chest, then cascaded down in streams of gold and purple at the skirt. She wore no sleeves and the top of the dress was cut enticingly low. Around her slender neck she wore a tight gold choker, also hung with small glittering swords. It was all I could do to keep my hands off her, instead clenching them hard at my sides.

I had never wanted anybody so badly in my life. In fact, each time my eyes fell on her impossibly beautiful face, I questioned whether I had wanted anything at all as much as I wanted Bella. The thought of her with someone else made rage flood through my veins. She was mine.

Only, she wasn't. And when she found out what I was hiding from her, the truth about where she had come from, she never would be mine.

I had to stop her finding out. Eris was close to the truth, I could see it in her eyes, hear it in her teasing voice. Would she tell Bella? Was her fondness for me stronger than her need to create chaos?

I knew the answer to that already. Nothing was greater than Eris' desire to create chaos.

Zeeva would find out from her master, my mother, soon enough. Hera knew exactly where Bella had come from. But for some reason, she had not yet shared what she knew with the cat. Why not? And why had she not spoken to me? A flutter of concern for her shimmied through me.

I had long since learned that my mother loved me no more or less than all the subjects she ruled over, and significantly less than she loved my father, Zeus. My parents were stronger than I, and affection within families did not function in Olympus like it did in Bella's world. They were my superiors, authorities that I bowed down to, and not a lot more. I respected that, and always had. War and Chaos were born of the same power but unlike my sister, I knew the importance of order and respect. It was one of the things that made me so strong.

You are not strong any more. You are weak without your power. The voice inside me clawed at my mind, just as it had since the fight with my father. But something was different now.

It was true that I was powerless. Dependent on a woman who should hate me. Dependent on a woman I was becoming obsessed with.

But a slow rumble rolled through me, starting in my gut and spreading through my chest, up into my throat. A collection of those invasive new emotions.

Excitement. Anticipation. *Nervousness.*

How had I never known these sensations before? We might fail to steal the tooth. I might fall into a pit of creatures who would send me mad for eternity. I might be forced into a panic so intense that I ended up a trophy in Panic's collection. The Lord we planned to cross was as strong as Bella and I were, though he wasn't sure enough of that to test it yet.

But the thrill of that knowledge was intoxicating. I had spent hundreds of years doling out punishment, instilling the need for confrontation into my citizens, overseeing battles and fights that were sometimes breathtaking in their beauty. But despite the strengthening surge of power those events gave me, I had been endlessly unsatisfied. Nothing had stirred so fiercely inside me, brought the light of every moment to life, or relieved me of my mental inhibitions like mortality had. My mind was racing with thoughts I would never have permitted before, almost all of them ending with Bella wrapped around me, her heart beating in time with mine, lost to the fire and the drums, and the pleasure. I would never have permitted thoughts like these before, dismissing them as useless fantasies that did not further my goals or make me stronger or give me power. But now, I reveled in them. Because for the first time in my long life, there was a chance I would only ever experience them in my imagination. I might die before I got what I wanted.

I was not mistaking the intense feeling of being alive for a desire for death. I would do whatever it took to live, and I knew that it would take something truly mighty to end my life. Power or none, I was still the ancient and immeasurably experienced God of War. But even that confidence was new, since having my power stolen. Aphrodite had said I was a wolf without its fangs or claws and I had believed her. But now, Bella was making me wonder. She had survived and fought her way through so much, more than she even knew, with barely a hint of power. She had become an incredible fighter, with an unbreakable spirit, without being a goddess. Was there a chance I could do the same?

With any luck, I wouldn't have to find out. We would win the Ares Trials, and I would receive the Trident of power. Even better, my father would come to his damn senses and return my own power to me.

Thinking about the future made my eyes flick automatically to Bella. If she found out what I had done, she would not feature in my future. In fact, she could ensure there was no future for me at all.

She realized I was looking at her, and her gaze locked on mine. All sensible thoughts fled, replaced by a single, burning need. She was mine.

I would have to make her understand, have to make her forgive me. She was mine.

. . .

"Right, I'm ready now. Let's go." Eris stepped out of the bathroom, and I took a deep breath as subtly as I could manage, setting my churning thoughts aside and focusing on the task at hand.

It was time to put on a show.

20

BELLA

I thought that I knew to what to expect when Eris flashed us to the ball. I'd been to too many of these soirees now. But what I saw when we arrived took my breath away.

The arched ballroom was in a castle that was about as far from crumbling as it could get. It reminded me of a church, with high vaulted ceilings and a mezzanine floor than ran around the perimeter of the room ten feet above the floor. The forest existed within the walls of the castle, every stone surface adorned with creeping vines that flowered with buds and petals the color of blood. The vines wrapped themselves around the balustrades that lined the grand central staircase leading up to the mezzanine, then wound their way across parts of the flagstone covered floor, and up the arched ceilings.

The room was filled with people and creatures, of every color, shape and size I could imagine, and all were dressed magnificently. The serving satyrs and tree dryads I'd seen before were moving between groups, carrying trays covered in drinks and exotic looking snacks.

My brow furrowed as I stared at the ceiling. The vines were moving. Some sort of string instrument sounded as I watched, then many more joined in and I gasped as a woman melted out of the foliage high above us. A smattering of applause sounded, and then the music drowned it out, an operatic voice joining the string instruments as the woman began to lower herself to the ground using a vine that appeared to be doing her bidding. When she was halfway down, she stopped, reached out her other hand, and a vine that had been wrapped around the mezzanine railings uncoiled itself and whipped toward her.

She had dark skin and wore a glittering green sheath dress that showed off insanely lovely legs. Slowly, she began to swing between the two vines. Then, when the music hit a high note, she let go, flipping herself high into the air, then turning mid-flight, her skirt whipping out and sparkling as she spun. I felt my hand go to my mouth as she fell, but before she even got close to the ground, more vines flew toward her, and she caught them, revolving and twirling in the air.

It was like the most magical Cirque du Soleil ever, and I could have watched her acrobatics for hours, but I felt a tug on my elbow.

When I looked down, Poseidon, Hades and Persephone were standing in front of me. A wave of deference washed over me, the need to worship these almighty beings built into their very presence. I bowed.

"You are doing well, both of you," said Poseidon. His white hair was pulled back into a tail, and he had a gleaming trident in his hand. He wore a toga, but I could see leather and metal strapping where the fabric parted over his chest.

"What happened with the dragon?" Hades' voice came from his smoky form.

"That is between the dragon and us," said Ares. Poseidon's expression tightened a moment, but then relaxed.

"As you wish. We have been searching for Zeus' ship. We believe you are right; he's using Guardian magic to mask himself, just as the Guardians mask magic in the mortal world."

"Will that harm the Guardians?" I asked quickly.

Poseidon looked at me. "I don't know."

"I believe not. He needs them alive and healthy to use their magic." Hades' spoke with a softness I didn't expect, and I nodded gratefully at him.

"How come I saw Joshua's body dead in my world, but alive on those stone beds?" I asked. The question had been lurking at the back of my mind for days.

"Guardians, along with a few other beings, can move their soul between multiple bodies. They can't flash, so they keep hosts in Olympus and the mortal world, so that they can move between the two."

"Like clones?" The idea was crazy.

Persephone nodded. "Weird, isn't it?"

Before I could agree, Poseidon spoke. "My general

came across the demon once, but there's been no sign of Zeus."

"I assume they didn't capture it, or this would be over." Ares' voice was level.

Poseidon shook his head tersely. "No. She is strong."

Thinking about the demon made my skin feel like it was burning. If Poseidon's general couldn't capture her, what hope did I have?

"Ares, there's something you need to know." Poseidon's tone was awkward, and I suddenly felt like I shouldn't be present for this conversation.

"What?" he asked, standing taller, his demeanor all arrogance that I wasn't sure I believed.

"We may be wrong but... My general reported that the demon used power she shouldn't have. Power she recognized."

Every muscle in Ares' body stiffened. "That's... That's unlikely."

Poseidon's eyes softened. "Ares, I'm sorry. You taught my general yourself, and have sparred with her many times since. She was certain it was your power signature."

An uneasy, sick feeling gurgled through my center, and I was sure it was coming from Ares somehow, but I didn't fully understand what the gods were talking about. Ares looked at me.

"It sounds like my father may have given my power to the demon."

~

I wished I could see Ares' face behind his helmet. All I had access to was his eyes though, and they were as cold and hard as I'd ever seen them.

"I must speak with Eris. Thank you for telling me this," Ares said stiffly, and the other two gods nodded and turned away. Persephone caught my eyes.

"You're doing great," she said with a small smile.

"Thanks," I said, then turned to follow Ares as he stamped toward where his sister was chatting with a pretty man with white wings.

"Eris, I need a word. Now," Ares snapped, yanking her back by the shoulder. A wave of tingling heat washed over me as she turned, fury in her eyes. It faded though as she saw his expression, a smile pulling at her purple-painted lips instead.

"Oh my, what's got into you?" she asked, as he pulled her away from the man, stopping when we reached a narrow Greek style column with warm orange flames flickering on the top.

"You knew. You knew what Zeus had done with my power." His words dripped with icy fury, but I felt no pull in my gut.

Eris' smile slipped for a microsecond. "Yes. I told you I would trade the information, and you refused me. That's your problem, not mine."

"I thought I could trust you," he snarled.

"Then you're a bigger fool than I thought you were," she answered, her eyes as hard as his.

There was an abrupt yank on my power, and Ares shone bright gold.

"If you still want my help tonight, I'd advise calming down, little brother."

Ares' eyes flicked to mine, and he let go of Eris' shoulder. "I will be back in ten minutes, and then we shall put our plan into action." Without waiting for an answer, he strode away. I moved to go after him, but Eris grabbed my elbow as I turned.

"Let him cool off. You need him at full strength tonight."

"I'm assuming that it's pretty bad to give a god's power to someone else?" I asked her.

Her eyes dipped to the floor before she answered me. "It shouldn't be possible. Only a being as powerful as Zeus could do it and it breaks one of the few rules the gods have." She let out a sigh. "A god's power is part of them. It's the height of fucked up to steal power and then give it to someone else."

"And it was his own father who did it," I said quietly.

"Yeah."

All the angry pride she'd projected at her brother was gone, and I really wanted to believe that she hadn't told Ares because she knew it would upset him. But then why would she pretend to be such a bitch about it?

"Can we still trust you to help us tonight?" I asked her quietly.

"I said I would, and I will. I'm quite used to my brother's temper tantrums." She rolled her eyes and swigged from her glass, and I buried the desire to defend him.

"Good," I said, and headed into the crowd to find the God of War.

"You know, in London we would call your sister a twat. And your dad a total and utter fuckwit."

Ares turned away from the vine covered wall he was staring at to face me. I had expected to see fiery fury in his eyes but there was a hollowness in them that caused a desperate pang of sadness to lance through my heart.

"My father has no duty to treat me differently than anyone else in Olympus. He has broken too many rules already, what is one more to further his plan? I was once going to let Hippolyta die, because the rules of a game demanded it." I was certain I could hear shame in his voice.

"Do you regret that?"

"I am glad she lived."

"That's not an answer."

"Regret is the wrong word. I wonder though, if there is a better way to live my life."

I may only have been around this guy a short time, but the impact of his words were not lost on me. The ancient, angry, arrogant god I had met in London would never have uttered that sentence.

"We'll get your power back from her. I'll help you get it back. I swear."

The hollow look in his eyes flickered, then in a heartbeat was replaced with an *inferno*. My lips parted in surprise as he pulled off his helmet, before closing the distance between us in one stride.

"You are changing me, Bella," he breathed, his hand moving to the back of my head, and pulling my mouth so close to his that I felt his hot breath mingle with my own. "I need you." His words were the most intense aphrodisiac imaginable. Nobody had ever needed me. And sure as fuck nobody like Ares.

The drums of war leaped to life in my ears, no slow and steady build up this time - they were as fast and hard as my heart felt in my chest. As Ares' lips claimed mine liquid fire rushed through my body, building deliciously in my core. I kissed him back as desperately as he kissed me, reveling in his hunger as his tongue flicked against mine, and he pulled me as close to him as I could get, as though any gap between us was intolerable.

A faint part of my brain became aware that we were very much in public, and I moved back an inch, sliding a sideways glance at the room.

Every guest in the ballroom was staring at us. My gaze found the three Lords of War in the crowd easily, but thankfully Aphrodite was nowhere to be seen. I took a massive breath as Ares stood straight.

"Is this not a celebration? Let us dance!" My mouth fell open as the God of War roared the words, and a vibrant tune started up immediately in response. Mercifully, most of the guests turned away from us, finding partners quickly and spinning around the room in elegant maneuvers.

"Well, that's one way to get rid of them," I muttered.

"The Lords will be over very soon," Ares said, tipping my chin up to look into my eyes.

"Aphrodite isn't here," I said.

"No." His expression changed, a darkness taking his eyes a moment, and words tumbled from my lips.

"Do you love her?" I totally failed to keep my emotion from the words. I was well beyond playing it cool. He knew I wanted him, and it was pointless to try to hide it. But if he still wanted Aphrodite, I needed to know now. How could he not? She was the freaking Goddess of Love, the most beautiful being in the world.

"No."

Blissful relief crashed over me and I realized just how much I had feared how far Aphrodite's hold on him went. I couldn't respect a man who let a woman treat him like she had - and I wanted so, so badly to let myself respect Ares. The glimpses of him under the armor, both physically and mentally, made me desperate for more. Tiny hints of his sense of humor, his tenderness, his intelligence, were starting to take their place beside the awe I had for him as a warrior, and I knew I was at real risk of falling for him if I saw much more.

"Good," I said, and couldn't help the smile spreading across my face.

21

BELLA

"The Lords are coming," he said, then ducked down to pick up his helmet. With a shimmer and a tiny fizz in my gut, he turned it into the headband and fixed it on his forehead, before reaching one arm around my waist and lifting my other hand in his, then twirling me around in something akin to a waltz.

"You dance?" I laughed with astonishment.

"When I need an excuse to be close to you, I dance," he said. His words caused a frisson of pleasure to flutter through my chest.

"And an excuse to avoid the Lords of War," I added, as we spun our way past them. I threw a sarcastic smile at the three of them over Ares' broad shoulder as we merged into the crowd of other dancers. Many of them looked at us, and I supposed that whipping his helmet off and kissing girls wasn't a usual activity for Ares at parties. I moved closer to him, almost possessively at the thought, wishing his armor wasn't blocking my skin from touching his. It was warm though. I drew on my power just enough to add half a foot to my height. Enough that I could press my mouth close to his neck.

"I want you out of this armor," I whispered into his throat, so quietly I wasn't even sure he would hear me.

I felt his arm tense around my waist, pulling me even tighter to him, then he twirled fast, making me giggle as he almost took me off my feet. When his eyes met mine as we slowed, his hunger was evident.

"This armor is the only thing keeping me from taking you right now," he growled. Heat flooded my core, and I felt every muscle in my body clench.

"Not all these lovely people?" I said, trying to keep my voice flirty instead of desperate, and raising it just enough that others could hear. "I'd much rather we were alone." That was the plan, as Eris had instructed us. Make it look like we couldn't keep our hands off each other, make it clear we were going somewhere to be alone together. But at that point, I wasn't speaking scripted lines. I'd have done anything to be alone with him.

He stared into my eyes as we danced to the cheerful song that I could barely hear over the beating drums. When he spoke, his lips didn't move and I realized only I could hear him. *This dragon better appreciate this damn tooth. Because this is the strongest test of my will power I have ever experienced.*

I bit down on my bottom lip and replied, wanting to push him. *I don't know what you mean? What's testing your will so bad, armor-boy?*

Desire flashed hungrily in his eyes. *"You. You are fucking irresistible."*

"You cursed," I whispered aloud, smiling from ear to ear. Ares wanted me just as much as I wanted him, and the knowledge was the most delicious thing in the world.

"It's your bad influence," he said, then his mouth claimed mine again, and just like the very first time we had kissed, that feeling of perfect rightness overwhelmed me. This was where I was meant to be, in Ares' arms.

The kiss was too short, but the raging inferno in Ares' eyes told me why. He hadn't been exaggerating, he really was struggling to contain himself. I moved out of his embrace and tugged him by the hand toward the grand staircase. He followed me, and I felt a glow of satisfaction at the surprised murmurs of the other guests. Ares was mine, and they all knew it. The staircase was lined with a moss green carpet that my gold high heels sank into, but I hardly noticed. All I was aware of was the hulking god's finger entwined with mine as he moved behind me. Yes, this was all part of the plan. But holy hell, it could so easily turn into more.

There were guests all along the long mezzanine floor, some leaning over the railings, some watching the acrobat, entranced. A few turned our way, then snickered behind their hands as we half-raced to the nearest finely-carved wooden doorway. There was another staircase through it, this one narrow and made of paler wood. I had already known that, because Zeeva had told us how to get to the north-east tower before we left.

Up two more flights of steps, take a long corridor to the left, go through a door that would lead us to a small outside bridge, which would take us to the tower we needed. Once in, we had to find a tapestry of a kraken, which hid a passageway leading to more stairs. The trick staircase that could kill us.

We half ran up the two longs flights of steps, and I almost gasped with relief to see the corridor was completely empty, both to the left and right. I turned to Ares, and with a pull in my gut his armor vanished, his headband glowing brightly for a moment. Then he closed the gap between us, pressing me hard into the vine-covered wall behind me. He pushed one hand into my hair, the other caressing my cheek.

"You are intoxicating," he breathed, as the drums beat.

"So are you," I replied, and he was. I reached up to touch his hard, stubbled jaw, his beautiful eyes mesmerizing.

"I need you. Now."

Fuck, was I ready. The ache of need in my core was almost painful, my lungs barely working properly as my chest heaved. "I'm yours."

With a noise between a groan and a snarl, Ares dropped his head, and kissed my throat, wrapping one arm around my waist and pulling me tight to him. I let out a moan as I felt his hardness through the thin material of his slacks, then fumbled to get my hands between our bodies, needing to touch him. He pulled back a little and kissed lower, across my collarbone and down towards my tightly encased breasts. My skin was alive with sensation, and every time his lips landed I could feel sparks of pleasure run straight to my sex, making my legs feel weak.

My hands reached the waist of his pants, and I couldn't resist running them up over his solid abs. He was so hard, so strong, so fierce. So perfect.

"God," I moaned, and he moved again, kissing me on the mouth hard. With an anticipation that blew the excitement I usually felt before any fight totally out of the water, I reached my hand into his pants. I don't know what noise I made as his kiss intensified, but I had sure as fuck never made it before.

Perfect was an understatement.

"Please," I gasped, breaking the kiss and tugging his glorious length free of the fabric of his pants. "I need you." He growled something unintelligible, then lifted me off the ground with the arm he had around my waist. I squeaked as my hand was pulled from him, then wrapped my legs around his solid middle, pulling at my skirts so that there was no fabric between us. I wound my own arms around his neck and tipped my head back against the wall as I felt the tip of him against my aching wetness.

"Ares," I breathed, barely even aware I was speaking. I had never needed anything so badly in my life. I'd have given up anything, anything at all, for this moment.

The ground shook beneath us, the wall I was pressed against rumbling loudly.

"*You two need to move, now!*" Eris' voice lanced through my passion, and Ares froze.

"Shit! Shit, shit, shit!" I cursed as he looked at me, clearly as unwilling to stop what we were about to do as I was. Then the floor actually lurched, and Ares stumbled to the side. I swung my legs to the ground to try to help steady us, my face and body aflame as I brushed against him, but then we were tipping the other way, and it was all I could do to stay on my feet. With a small shimmer Ares' armor was back in place, and grabbing for each other's hands we began to run down the corridor.

"He knows we're here," said Ares, his voice as strained as my tingling body felt.

"Asshole," I spat.

"I thought that was reserved for me?" Ares called, his pace quickening as the corridor lurched again in the opposite direction, flinging us toward the opposite wall. We were too quick though, both of us keeping our footing as we raced on, our hands still locked together.

"Not anymore."

At the end of the foliage-covered corridor was a steel door, and we hurled ourselves against it as the floor achieved its most violent lurch yet.

"Is the whole castle moving?" I panted, as we both tugged at a massive ornate door handle, my feet scrabbling to keep me upright as the floor moved.

"I don't know. This is locked." Ares let go of my hand, and an instant sense of despair gripped me. His eyes darted to mine, confirming he felt it too, before he pulled his sword from the sheath at his waist that had appeared with his magic armor. I let him draw on my power as he slammed the blade down onto the handle.

The metal severed from the door, and I leaned forward to tug out the mechanism inside that was keeping it locked. The second the door swung open freezing air washed over me, and I was looking out at a stone bridge being hammered by relentless rain. A medieval-looking stone tower was attached to the other end of the bridge, which had no sides or railings. I felt my stomach churn as the corridor we were still standing in lurched to the other side, but the bridge stayed still. It wasn't the whole castle moving, just the tower we were in.

Before fear could get the better of me, or I could be thrown on my ass by the lurching corridor, I stepped out onto the bridge.

"Fuck, it's cold!" I yelled, as freezing rain pelted down on me. I took a step forward and my heel instantly slid on the sopping-wet stone. I ducked, pulling off both my shoes, and as I straightened a huge gust of wind hit me. My heart leaped into my throat as I teetered, clutching my shoes in one hand and waving my other arm for balance. I was just about to let go of the shoes and try to fling myself to the stone, when I felt Ares' massive hand close around my elbow, catching me. "Thank you," I gasped, heart hammering against my ribs.

"Move," the god barked in reply, and for once I did as I was told, putting one bare foot in front of the other as fast as I dared, Ares never letting go of me.

Thankfully the door on the other side wasn't locked and I wrenched it open and half threw myself inside, out of the horrendous rain. Ares followed me in fast, slamming the door shut behind me. We were at the bottom of another staircase, this one a wide spiral shape. The vines were less here, only sprawling across the low ceiling, and everything was lit dimly by glowing balls of green light that seemed embedded into the rock itself.

"I'm soaked," I said quietly, leaning against the wall and getting my breath, pushing strands of wet hair back from my face. It felt like the crazy-gorgeous headdress Eris had wrapped around it all had held it pretty well, all things considered.

"You can use your power to dry yourself. It's like using your healing power, but imagine it hotter instead."

I looked at Ares, wanting to ask him to do it for me. Better still, I wanted him to take all my wet clothes off and warm me up in a different way entirely. But there was no question of that now. Panic knew we were somewhere that we weren't supposed to be, so we were already on borrowed time. As soon as I thought of the Lord of War, I felt his presence, an urgent agitation at the back of my mind.

"He's trying to make contact with us," said Ares. "Don't let him."

I nodded, picturing my horse shield automatically. The presence diminished. "We'd better move," I said. "Zeeva said we need to look for a tapestry with a kraken on it."

"Let's hurry. I want this over with."

I knew exactly what he meant. The thrill of the heist was now nothing compared to the promise our bodies held one another. Although the extra bout of adrenaline our dash through the castle had stirred up wasn't doing me any harm. I knew I was glowing, I could see it on my skin. I was as alive as I'd ever felt, overflowing with energy.

Get the tooth, take it to Dentro, fuck the God of War senseless.

This had the potential to be a freaking excellent night.

22

BELLA

There were lots of tapestries hanging in the wide stairwell, and nearly all of them depicted fearsome looking monsters. It didn't take us long to find an image showing a giant octopus type creature, dragging a ship that was hovering twenty feet above the surface of the ocean down toward a watery end. It was heavy as hell, but we managed to pull it down between us, revealing an unnervingly tiny tunnel.

"Zeeva didn't mention it was this small," I said, eying the dark entrance.

"To her, it probably isn't small."

"I've seen her in big cat mode," I said, pulling a face. "She's not as tiny as you might think."

"Do you want to go first?" Ares asked me.

I nodded, then dropped to my knees. A faint smell was coming from the tunnel, but not an unpleasant one. It was a sort of smoky, tangy scent that I thought I recognized. "If this tower starts lurching around from side to side while I'm in there, I will not be happy," I said, looking up at Ares over my shoulder.

"Hopefully it is a defense unique to the last tower."

"Hopefully." I tried to keep the doubt from my voice, and leaned forward onto my hands.

The tunnel was shorter than I had expected it to be, and only properly dark for a few seconds, until it angled up sharply and light poured in from the other end. It was tiring moving up so steeply, but the stone was rough enough to keep a good grip on, and the pleasant smell made the work easier. When I crawled out of the end I found myself at the bottom of yet another staircase, but I could tell immediately that this one was different. There was no doubt in my mind that it was the trick staircase Zeeva had told us about.

It was huge, each step easily big enough for me to lie down on. And it wasn't tall either, only about twenty steps high, a innocuous looking wooden door at the top. Vines snaked their way across the ceiling here too, and coiled around the frame of the door, but they stayed clear of the stone steps. More green light glowed from the rock, mingling with my own gold glow. Ares emerged from the tunnel behind me as I got cautiously to my feet. As soon as I was at my full height I saw that the wide steps had carvings on them, but they seemed to blur every time I tried to focus.

"This feels wrong," Ares said, and I nodded in agreement. There was a kind of bad-shit vibe coming from the stone, like that feeling when the skies cloud over and it gets cold suddenly and you want to be somewhere else.

"Can you see what's carved onto the steps?" I asked him.

"No. The images keep moving." We both moved warily closer to the bottom step. The more I tried to work out the drawing, the more the lines seemed to leap about, evading me.

"Stay still," I snapped, and miraculously, they did. I looked slowly at Ares, my eyebrows arched. "Did I just do that?" I whispered.

"Maybe the magic here obeys war," he said, then turned to the stairs. I felt a little tug as he spoke, apparently to the stairs. "All false steps should reveal themselves now!" he ordered. Nothing happened, and a tiny snort of laughter escaped me.

"What did you expect, talking to a staircase?"

Ares glared at me. "Do you have any better ideas?" I leaned forward, peering at the now clear image on the lowest step. It showed a helmet similar in style to Ares' with a big plume on it, and a wreath underneath it.

I looked at the carving on the next step. It was a lion's head, its mouth open in a snarl, teeth bared. The step after that had nothing carved on it at all, and the one after that had a silhouette of a woman with a severe haircut, and a snake. I couldn't see higher than that without starting to move up the stairs.

"The pictures must mean something. That one with the lady looks like ancient Egyptian hieroglyphs. And her hair... She could be Cleopatra. She had something to do with a snake, I'm sure."

Ares looked at me as I screwed my face up in thought. "We do not have time for this."

"Well, unless you can fly, we'll have to work it out."

He paused, and I instantly got over-excited. "Can we fly? Please, please tell me we can fly!"

"No. Gods don't need to fly, they can flash."

"Oh." I felt my face fall. "And we can't flash in the castle," I said, putting my hands on my hips. Ares echoed my position, putting his own fists on his hips.

"No."

"OK then. Cleopatra. Do you have one of them in Olympus? Or is she just a mortal world person?"

"She is a minor deity in my realm."

"Ohh, I want to meet her!"

"Focus, Bella."

"Shit, yeah, sorry." I looked back to the carvings. "Does she have any war power?"

"Yes."

"OK. I don't know about the lion. You got any war lions in Olympus?"

"Yes. The Nemean Lion, though she is dead now. Killed during the Immortality Trials."

"OK, so the lion is Olympus only. What about the first picture? That could be you."

"No. The wreath means nothing to me."

"It could be Julius Caesar? He was a famous war general in my world."

Ares shrugged. "I have never heard of him. Athena manages the war and politics in the mortal world. I find it too... restrictive."

I sighed. "So there's no connection there, they're all different."

"Is your Julius Caesar character dead?"

"Long dead," I nodded.

"Like the Nemean Lion. Perhaps we should not stand on steps of warriors who have died?"

I took a deep breath. "It's worth a shot." Ares took a stride forward and I caught his armored arm. "Wait. Try putting something on the step first, as a test."

"Like what?"

I looked around the small space trying to find something that would weigh enough to trigger the trick step.

There was nothing. "Would any of my jewelry be heavy enough, do you think?" I asked him, touching the complicated headdress.

His eyes darkened, and I saw a flame spike in his irises as his eyes swept over me. "Your dress would be heavy enough."

"I am not taking my dress off," I said, giving him a hard look. "I'm already barefoot; if we get caught I'd rather I wasn't in my underwear."

"Then we test it with my life," he shrugged, and I could hear the teasing lilt in his voice.

"You're seriously saying that your life depends on me getting naked?"

"It would appear that way."

I rolled my eyes, then pulled the headdress from my head. My hair tumbled down my back as I worked it free, relieved to feel that the weight of it in my hands seemed to exceed how light it felt on my head. I laid it carefully on the lion step. Nothing happened.

"Take off your boots." I turned to Ares, holding my hand out.

"What?"

"They're not part of your magic armor are they?"

"No, but-"

"Then take them off," I commanded.

"You wish the God of War to tackle a great challenge with no shoes on?"

I lifted my skirt to my knees and wiggled my own bare toes at him. "Yup. Alongside the shoe-less Goddess of War."

There was a long pause, then Ares bent at the waist. "You have a power over me, woman," he muttered.

"Well, it wasn't working up until today," I said. "You have point-blank refused to do anything I've asked you before." He straightened, having tugged both his massive boots off. I looked down at his simple black stocking socks. When I looked back at his face, his eyes were serious.

"I mean it, Bella. I have given up trying to fight it. You do have a power over me."

My face heated with both pleasure and awkwardness.

"I have all the power," I grinned at him, trying to make light of the tension. "That's why I'm here, remember? War-magic battery?"

He shook his head and held out his boots. As soon as I added them to my headdress, the step made a loud cracking sound, then turned completely transparent. Alarm skittered down my spine as the sound of buzzing welled up loud in the small stone room and the boots and headdress fell clean through the step.

Fuck that. I did not want to be standing on one of

those any time soon. But the only way was up. We had promised Dentro, and we were not letting him down. I steeled myself, drawing on the flaming ball of power under my ribs to steady my nerves. My trepidation was instantly replaced with an earnestness to succeed that I knew bordered on dangerous. Every victory comes at a cost, I reminded myself, as I turned to Ares.

"I think your boots were heavy enough on their own," I told him. "That was a waste of a damn fine piece of jewelry."

23

ARES

"Do you think the blank step is safe?" I asked Bella.

"Must be. Nobody could reach the fourth step from here. Unless you were a giant."

"Shame we don't have more boots to test it out." I raised an eyebrow at her and she poked her tongue out at me. My body reacted instantly, my arousal unstoppable.

"Put that away, or Dentro will remain toothless," I growled. Pink flushed her cheeks, and she shifted her weight.

With a wrench, I turned away form her and surveyed the step without a carving. "If I fall, do you think you can catch me before the oxys get me?" I asked her.

"Catch you how?"

"You can make an air cushion to bounce me back out. Or send out whips. We can conjure up most weapons with our power." I was becoming comfortable calling it 'our' power, which was remarkable given how I had felt just a week earlier.

"Seriously, why didn't you teach me this shit before?"

"Just picture using the weapon as you draw on your power and it'll appear. It won't be anything like as strong as *Ischyros*, but it will function. You seem to learn fast. I trust you."

She nodded at me, expression resolute. With a quick breath I took a stride long enough to take me to the third step. My heart thudded in my chest as my weight settled, and Bella whooped. The step was holding. I turned to her, holding out my hand and helping her jump to join me when she took it.

I had expected to feel more confident with every correct guess, but that was not the case. Every time we hovered over a step I couldn't help thinking about what would happen if Bella was stung by the oxys, and my chest clenched with apprehension.

It took us much longer than I'd have liked to work out who all the little carved drawings were, but between us we prevailed.

"You know, I could do with a drink," Bella breathed when we finally reached the un-carved section of stone before the plain door.

"It's not over yet." I eyed the door handle suspiciously. Zeeva had said we needed war power to open it.

"You are stronger than me. I think you should try and open it."

"You're just saying that so that if it does something nasty it hits me instead of you," she teased.

"Never," I said, emotion flashing through my veins, and my hand reaching for hers protectively. "I would never risk your life for my own." The words were out before I had even thought them, and her surprise was evident.

"Really?"

I nodded. I didn't know when it had happened, exactly, but I knew that I had spoken the truth. When we had been drowning, and the awful realization that only one of use could use enough power to gain immortality, my instincts had made the decision for me. I wouldn't risk her life for mine.

And that fact directly contradicted everything I thought I had known about the Goddess of War for centuries. It challenged everything that had led me to make the decisions I had made all that time ago.

I needed time and space to work this out, to replay those ancient events and understand how I could have got it so wrong. I needed to talk to my mother.

That time was not now though. All I could do now was give in to the fact that Bella had utterly invaded my heart.

"Why?" she whispered, her eyes burning with emotion.

"I wouldn't be able stop myself if I wanted to. I believe we are bound."

She opened her mouth, then closed it again,

multiple times. "So... You don't want to feel like this? You just can't help it?" There was an edge of pain in her voice and it felt like I was being stabbed in the gut. I reached for her, drawing her close, running my hand down her soft cheek.

"I didn't know it was even possible for me to feel like this," I told her. "I would trade it for nothing in the whole of Olympus."

A smile, true and warm, lit her face, and she stood up on her bare tiptoes to kiss me softly. "I'm going to need you to say more things like that to me later. When we've got this damn tooth."

"It would be my pleasure."

Bella grinned, then looked down at the handle. It was made from the same rich-colored wood as the door and looked like it had once been carved into something, but years of wear had rubbed the shape away. That same uneasy feeling that I had experience on entering the room coiled around me, making my skin crawl.

"Wait," I said. "Let's do it together. Combine our strength."

A look of relief flickered across Bella's face. "Sure. Good plan. On the count of three?" I nodded.

Together, we clasped our right hands on the handle.

"Three, two, one."

24

BELLA

All the hairs on my skin stood on end, my scalp prickling. The door was moving, but barely by millimeters. My stomach shimmied and fluttered and my lungs seemed to expand in my chest, despite feeling less full of air. I pushed harder, feeling Ares do the same, but the door continued its minuscule crawl.

"Do we need to do war stuff?" I hissed. "It'll take a fucking week to open the door at this rate."

"I don't know. Draw on your war power and let's try," Ares replied, and his voice had the tiniest hit of unsteadiness in it.

"Are you feeling as weird as I am?" I asked, looking sideways at him, but somehow reluctant to draw my attention from the door handle for more than a second. It was as though my hand was glued to it.

"I feel peculiar, yes."

I dug inside myself, finding the burning well of

power hot and ready. I blew out a breath, and pictured the mounted version of me on the battlefield.

The moment I got the image in my head, the door moved faster under our weight. But the uneasy prickling instantly became a tsunami of panic.

I was drowning. I was in the pool again, the tentacles wrapped around me, but Ares' golden glow wasn't lighting the pitch dark water and I was being dragged down, down, down. I couldn't breathe, my head was filled with pain, my lungs were burning as an invisible band around my middle crushed the breath, the life, the soul out of my body. I was trapped, and I was going to die.

"Bella!" Ares' voice sounded in the distance, and the vision changed. I wasn't drowning anymore. He was. He was drowning and I would have to watch him die because I had the all of the power. I had the immortality. Only one of us could live forever and I would be the reason for the fierce warrior god's death.

I would kill the only man who had a chance of caring about me, understanding me. *Loving me.*

I had to watch him die.

Panic overwhelmed me completely, and I could hear myself screaming and thrashing as my limbs went numb, but I couldn't stop.

"Ares!" I screamed, as his body floated lifelessly in the inky water. My mouth filled with water, my eyes burning along with my chest.

.   .   .

Pain shocked through my whole body as though I'd slammed into something solid, totally at odds with the underwater vision that was dominating my mind.

When I blinked, the pool was gone, replaced by pale stone just inches from my eye. The tangy taste of blood in my mouth dragged me fully from the horrendous vision and I realized I was lying flat on the stone floor. Pain spiked from where my cheek must have hit the stone, and my ribs and shoulder felt as though they'd been hit by a truck as I tentatively tried to move. Residual images of Ares' dead body kept drifting across my vision, and my pulse was still racing at a hundred miles an hour. My chest hurt every time I took a ragged breath, and I didn't know if it was the panic, or true injury.

"Ares?" I tried to call his name, but the pain of moving my jaw brought tears to my eyes. Something was broken. *"Ares?"* I tried again, in my head this time.

"I'm here. Are you hurt?" His mental voice was tense.

"Yes."

"Heal yourself, quickly."

Shit, of course I could heal myself. The intensity of the vision had left me slow and fuzzy, and I reached inside myself, instructing my power to fix whatever was broken. Warm tingles shot out from my center, and my ribs hurt like hell for a split second, before I felt as though I could breathe properly again. Then my shoulder burned white hot, and I gulped down more air as the feeling of wrongness in my torso lessened. Next my face heated, and when it stopped I lifted my head a fraction. There was no pain.

I pushed myself up onto my hands and knees, testing my body before looking around myself.

"Ares!" He was lying beside me, and his face looked in worse shape than mine had felt.

"This is why I wear a helmet," he croaked inside my head. There was no way he could have moved his mouth. He looked as though he had been flung at the stone with the force of a hurricane, blood pooling under the side of his head that was smashed into the floor. I scrabbled over to him and laid my hands on his armor. I felt him pull on my power and I let him take it, trying somehow to send more through our connection.

"What happened?" I whispered. I was still reeling from the vision, and now, seeing him like this, bleeding and broken... The thought of something happening to him, of losing him, was unbearable. Somewhere along this crazy fucking journey, I had fallen for him. It wasn't just sex. It wasn't just desire. This was serious.

"I think the door opened, and we fell through."

"Fell? How fucking hard did we fall?" I could feel tears dangerously close to spilling from my eyes. He moved, just a little, but enough that I could see the crushed flesh on his face was glowing. *Healing.*

He was OK. He would be OK.

"We survived," he said, this time moving his lips, saying the words aloud. "So, I think we should take this as a victory."

"I like your thinking," I told him, stroking my hand down the undamaged side of his face, trying to get my shit together and contain my churning emotions. "We fucking showed that door who's boss." He gave a forced chuckle. "I... I had a vision," I said, quietly.

"Me too. One that would induce the power of Panic."

I nodded. "We were back in the pool in the forest."

"It wasn't real, Bella. Put it out of your mind." He rolled slowly onto his back, a shuddering breath making his armor move. There wasn't a dent in it. The force of whatever had caused us to slam into the floor had broken my shoulder and ribs but Ares' armor was solid.

"I'm sorry you didn't have your helmet on," I said.

"I'd happily have my face smashed up if it means I can kiss you at any opportunity," he said, his eyes closed as the skin over his cheek and jaw knitted itself back together as I watched.

"That's actually quite a romantic thing to say," I said. "Under the circumstances." I leaned over, and placed a tiny, gentle kiss on his lips. I felt the draw on my power fade as he glowed briefly, then opened his eyes, reaching a hand up and running it through the loose curls of my hair that were hanging down over him.

"I am healed," he said softly. "Thank you." I moved so that he could sit, and for the first time noticed the rest of the room we were in.

The evil-bastard door appeared to have closed behind us, and we were in the entrance way to a long hall. Two rows of pedestals ran down either side of the hall, lit by bright flickering flames that hung upside down from the low ceiling above them. Vines and branches covered the walls behind the pedestals, and the firelight made them look alive, as though they were crawling across the stone with purpose. From my position on the floor, I couldn't make out anything on top of the closest pedestals, only that whatever was in them was encased inside a glass dome, like the rose in Beauty and the Beast.

"We're in," I said, standing up carefully. "We made it into the trophy room."

"Are you fully healed?" Ares' voice was filled with concern as he stood too.

"Yes, I'm fine. I've spent a lifetime having to move slowly after having the shit kicked out of me. It'll take me a while to get used to being able to just bounce back up."

Rage flashed through Ares' beautiful eyes. "I shall murder all those who ever kicked the shit out of you," he growled.

I laughed. "That's very sweet, armor-boy, but most of them were paid to do so, in a fighting ring. I signed up for it."

His eyes narrowed. "You fought in pits?"

"Sort of, I guess. But as I said, I was paid. And I liked proving the people who bet against me wrong."

"Is that why you care about the slaves?" he asked quietly.

"No, I care about the slaves because it's fundamentally wrong to take somebody's freedom from them," I said. "Look, we can talk about this later. Let's find this tooth and get the fuck out of here, before the Lords show up." I left off the rest of the sentence that was bouncing around in my head. *Don't remind me of the things I don't like about you.* I knew I would have to deal with the serious differences in opinion and nature Ares and I had. But there had to be a way through it. I knew he was capable of change; he had told me himself that I was affecting how he saw the world.

"My sister must be doing a good job of distracting them. It has been a long time since her warning."

"Yeah. I hope she's OK."

Ares pulled a face. "Eris is always OK. It is her victims who you should worry about."

"Hmmm. You make a good point. Right. Where's this tooth?"

I took a step down the hall, renewed determination to get the job done, pronto, flooding through me. So far, Panic's tower had not delivered the evening I was hoping for, but there was still time to rescue it.

25

BELLA

Some of the items under the glass domes in Panic's trophy room made Belle's rose look positively dull.

"What in the name of sweet fuck is that?" I breathed, staring at something that might have passed for a human hand, were it not for the hundreds of eyes and legs all over it. It was motionless on top of the pedestal, I presumed dead.

Ares stopped beside me, and his nose wrinkled in distaste. "I have no idea."

There were lots of pieces of jewelry, shining gems and pretty tiaras, and also many weapons. Ares was particularly enamored with a battle-axe made from gleaming bronze, but I tugged him further down the hall.

"We're here for the tooth. Don't get greedy. That's how they always get caught."

"Who gets caught?"

"Everyone. You know, in plays and movies."

"I don't know what you're talking about."

I sighed. "Nothing new there then. When this is all over, I'm taking you to the theater," I told him.

"Oh. Well, then I shall take you to a theater too."

"Excellent," I said, throwing him a smile.

Eventually, when we were three pedestals from the end of the hall, we reached a glass dome covering a sharp, yellowing tooth.

"Do you think that's it?" I asked, peering at it intently.

"It is certainly large enough."

"Let's check the last few, before we start smashing up the wrong one." Moving quickly, we scanned the few remaining trophies. When I reached the last two pedestals, something skittered over my skin, warm and electric, and I could smell smoke all of a sudden. The sound of steel clashing rang in my ears, and I frowned.

"Can you feel that?" It wasn't the Lords. In fact, I didn't think it was a bad feeling at all. Battle-cries echoed in the far distance, and the mounted version of me, sword raised high, galloped through my mind.

I looked at Ares, about to repeat my question, when I saw that his gaze was fixed on the pedestal in front of him.

The second my eyes fell on the object inside, I gasped aloud, my body filling with a heady surge of my new power.

It was a helmet. Similar in style to Ares' but the plume was purple, and it was smaller. The eye slits were larger though, and the cut out opened higher, so the wearer's mouth would be seen. I reached out as I stepped toward it, knowing for sure that this was not the first time I'd seen this helmet. Just like the shield with the horses, or *Ischyros* in true form. *I knew this helmet.*

"Ares?" My word came out as a question, and when he looked at me his eyes were full of pain and sorrow.

"We must take it," he said, his voice low and resolute. Despite my previous assertion that we take nothing but the tooth, I had no intention of arguing with him. I was connected to that helmet somehow, and at that moment I wanted little more than to free it from its glass prison.

"Yes, OK. But we get the tooth first."

He nodded, and we jogged back to Dentro's tooth, a sudden urgency to our movements.

Ares recognized the helmet too, I was sure of it.

The God of War drew his sword, and the sound of steel on steel set my heart racing faster. I pulled my flick-blade from where it was concealed between my breasts in the tight dress, sighing with pleasure as the weapon heated in my hand and transformed into the magnificent weapon it really was.

"On three again?" Ares asked me.

"Sure."

"Three, two, one!"

Together we arced our blades through the air, bringing them crashing down onto the glass. I poured my power into the sword, and let Ares draw as much as he wanted from the burning well inside me. As we made contact time slowed to a standstill, and the ringing of the weapons against the dome echoed through the stone room. Then, in a rush, the glass shattered completely, cascading onto the floor below. I reached out, scooping Dentro's massive tooth up, and tucking it under my arm.

A freezing wave of air blew through the room in a gust, carrying with it a distinct sense of despair.

"He knows we're here," Ares said, and I sprinted with him toward the helmet. My skin began to crawl again as the gust of air swirled harder, picking up my hair and skirts. I glanced over my shoulder as I reached the helmet's pedestal, breathing in sharply as I saw that the air was tightening into a tornado, and solidifying. It was Panic.

"He's here," I shouted, and turned, trying to raise my sword with my right arm and keep my hold on the awkward tooth with the other. An awful sense of doom was seeping into me, as though my skin was absorbing the power carried by Panic's presence. The sensation brought the visions of losing Ares in the pool dancing back in front of my eyes.

The crash of metal on glass snapped me back, and I focused as Ares pulled his weapon back from the blow he had just landed on the dome. It hadn't broken the glass, just left a widening crack.

"I need you," he barked, eyes wild. I raised *Ischyros*, and without a countdown this time, we slammed our swords into the dome in unison. My blow was awkward, but I channeled enough fear-fueled power into it that it worked, the glass splintering into a thousand pieces. Ares snatched up the helmet from amongst the shards, then I heard his voice bellow in my head.

"Eris! Help us!"

"Your sister has been detained, oh mighty one."

Panic's voice was like nails down a chalkboard, and all the hairs on my body stood on end as we both turned slowly.

He wasn't alone. Pain and Terror were standing behind him, and another wave of hopelessness crashed over me. Together they were stronger than us. If this came down to a fight, we would lose. And I had vowed to return the tooth to the magnificent enslaved dragon. I had to save him.

"You can't contain the Goddess of Chaos," Ares snorted, all panic and urgency gone from his voice. He sounded like he had zero fucks to give. I did my best to emulate him.

"Yeah, Eris does what she likes," I said.

A slow, creepy smile spread across Panic's face. He was dressed exactly like he owned a castle filled with plants. His outfit was medieval in style, britches and shirt and big leather boots, but it was all in shades of mossy green. "Not any more. I'm afraid her ongoing spat with Aphrodite seems to have come to a head."

Fuck. We were trapped. My power wasn't strong enough for Ares to flash us out of a no-flash-zone, and there were no windows or doors except the one they were blocking.

Panic's eyes flicked between the tooth under my arm and the helmet Ares was clutching. "I see now why Dentro let you go," he murmured. "Clever dragon. He'll pay for his deviousness." A shudder rippled down my spine as the temperature dropped even further.

"You're an asshole. That dragon deserves to be free," I spat.

"That dragon shouldn't have been careless enough to lose his tooth," Panic hissed back. "Now, give me back my property, and we'll pretend this never happened. We'll return to the ball and announce the last Trial." He held his hand out.

"Fuck off." There was no way I was handing over the tooth. He'd have to fight me for it, whether I could win or not. I felt a surge of hot energy, buffering me against his cold, unsettling presence.

"Then we will take it from you."

I threw up my shield as Ares spoke in my head. *"Do you trust me?"*

"Of course."

He pulled on my power, and I let him take it.

In a rush I felt my strength leaving me, the tooth becoming alarmingly heavy, *Ischyros* even more so. I felt my legs bend under the weight, and Panic's eyes lit up as he realized my shield was gone. A wall of air slammed into me, nearly toppling me, a hideous wailing noise riding with it. I almost dropped the sword and tooth to clap my hands over my ears, the sound was so unpleasant. Panic began to crawl its way up my chest, my throat, taking over, unstoppable.

Then I was jerked backwards as a huge arm wrapped around my waist, spinning me around.

"Run!" Ares yelled, and began to race toward the solid stone wall at the end of the hall.

I did as he said, wanting to scream at how slowly I was moving. All my usual speed and power was gone, and the weight of my sword and the tooth slowed me further. Heat flared from Ares, just ahead of me, then a fireball twice my height erupted from him. My mouth fell open, and I stumbled, then Panic's wailing tornado smashed into my back. I cried out as I tumbled forward, catching myself on my hands and knees as I hit the floor, the tooth and *Ischyros* clattering out of my hands.

I saw the fireball explode as it hit the stone wall, and threw one arm up in front of me, as though that would help shield me. A flaming shower of stone and burning chunks of vines came flying toward me, but hit an invisible wall, sliding harmlessly off. I looked up breathlessly as Ares, glowing the brightest gold, couched beside me, tugging me to my feet. I felt power begin to flow back into me, and I pulled gratefully at it, glorious strength flooding back into my muscles. I reached for *Ischyros* as Ares snatched up the tooth, then ran toward the exploded wall, me right behind him. There was a big, ragged hole blasted in the stone.

"Ready?" he shouted as Panic made a strangled sound behind us.

"Hell yes!" I yelled, and we launched ourselves out of the tower.

26

BELLA

My heart was in my throat as we fell through the cold air, rain hammering down so hard I could barely see.

"Shield!" I heard Ares yell, and I pictured my horse shield and tightened my grip on *Ischyros*. With an almighty crash, we hit something, but before I could work out what, the world flashed white.

I sucked in air, looking around desperately for Ares. We were back in the gloomy forest, even darker than the last time we'd been there, now that it was night.

Ares was standing beside me in the pouring rain, his eyes alive with excitement. I tried to focus on what was behind him, to check our surroundings, but he was glowing so bright, and I couldn't look away from him.

"I had no idea that running away could be so exhilarating," he breathed, before stepping toward me and kissing me briefly but oh so passionately. When he moved back the fire was dancing in his irises, his gaze piercing. "What else can you show me, that I didn't know?" He sounded genuinely amazed, as well as sexy as hell, and I didn't know if he was referring to his lack of immortality, his newfound emotion for me, or just sex. Maybe all three.

"Let's get this tooth to Dentro before Panic catches us up, and then we'll find out," I said, my voice abnormally husky.

"Bella, you've made me question everything," he said. "Everything. Please, tell me you know that I can change." There was a plea in his voice that was so at odds with the prideful god's usual tone, and my heart seemed to swell inside my chest.

"Yes. But you don't need to change, Ares. You just need to review some outdated attitudes."

"So... So you don't hold my bad decisions against me?"

He sounded almost fearful, and I cocked my head at him, the intensity of the emotion on his face surprising me. Was he talking about the way he ruled his realm? Or something else?

"We all make mistakes. And we can all try to fix them."

"Bella." He said my name as though it were an apology, pain filling his eyes, and I couldn't help frowning as the rain beat down on us.

"What? What's wrong?"

"I need you to know this, Bella. I need you to know it now."

"Know what?" My nerves were skittering now, a sick feeling swishing around inside me.

"I think I've fallen in love with you."

.   .   .

My heart skipped a beat as I stared at him. For a truly blissful second a sense of rightness slid over us, the rain and the awful forest and everything else shit in the world, fading to nothing. There was nothing but him, and the undeniable knowledge that we were meant to be together. We were two halves of the same thing.

Then agony seared through my head, and I screamed, dropping what I was holding and falling to my knees. My skull felt like it was being split in two, and I barely heard Ares shout over the pain.

A cackling laugh filled the air around us, then Aphrodite's voice rang between the trees, slicing through everything else. "Love, dear ones, is when my power works. Only when you say the words, can my curse come to life. Do you want to see what you have fallen for, Bella? Do you want to see just how savage your god can be?"

"No!" shouted Ares, and I lifted my head, eyes streaming with the pain, to see Ares begin to grow. The cord in my gut fired to life as he drew my power from me.

"Yes, Ares. If you truly love her, and you want her to love you back, she must see you at your worst."

His face was changing as I watched, the beautiful flames in his eyes gone, cold hard darkness replacing them. The air filled with the stench of blood, tangy and cloying, and the golden glow around him was turning red. He was ten feet tall now at least, and he was taking more of my power by the second. I tried to clamp down on the flow, to stop him, but as soon as I tried, he growled, an inhuman, awful sound. His pull got harder, and I cried out in frustration. Something flickered in his eyes, but then I heard Aphrodite laugh again, and his irises turned completely black.

"He's all yours, Bella."

I pushed myself to my feet, my strength diminishing fast. I pulled *Ischyros* with me, but when I tried to lift the sword I found it too heavy. A bolt of fear shot through me as I looked up at Ares.

He had doubled in size, and his red light cast eerie shadows on the forest around us.

"Ares, please. Stop taking my power." I saw nothing of him that I recognized in his black eyes as he looked down from where he towered above me. He took the gold headband off and it began to grow into his helmet, matching his size. Dizziness washed through me as he pulled it down over his head, and another, bigger, bolt of fear raced through me as I felt for the well of power inside me. It was too small. And getting smaller.

"Ares!" I tried again, louder. "Ares, don't drain my power!"

"Your power?" His voice was huge and booming, and totally alien. He stamped his foot as he looked down at me, his whole body beaming with the color of the plume on his helmet. "The power you wield is mine!" I barely had time to react as he kicked out with his bootless foot, throwing myself to the ground and rolling out of the way just in time.

"Ares, stop! It's me!"

"I am the God of War!" he roared, rain hammering

against his armor as he continued to grow, his height almost matching that of the trees around us. "You will bow to me! All will bow to me!" The sound of clashing of steel and galloping hooves rang through the air, then cannon fire and gunshots mingled with the noise. Abruptly the sounds were overcome by the screams of the dying, men and women wailing and crying.

"Stop!" My voice was rasping, and I could hear the tears in them.

This couldn't be happening.

The man who had just told me that he thought he loved me couldn't be the same man who towered over me now, emanating death. "Ares, please!"

"This is the true power of war," he bellowed. "You are not worthy of it. It must return to me." His voice was a savage growl as his cold, dead eyes locked on me, and I had no doubt what he would do next. Fatigue was dragging at my limbs, dark spots floating across my vision, the red-mist nowhere to be seen. I didn't have enough power left to fight him.

I felt like my chest was being cleaved apart, and it wasn't a physical wound. It was so much worse. The connection with Ares that had burned brighter within me the longer I was with him was gone. All that was left was the sickening feeling of him draining my power. There were two cords, two connections, I realized, eyes burning. One was power, running straight to the burning well of magic. But the other, now lifeless, ran straight to my soul.

A sob fought its way up and out of my throat. I

would have to run, before the man I was falling in love with tried to kill me.

Turning almost blindly, I felt the ground shake beneath my bare feet, then heard the sound of wood being wrenched apart.

"Enyo." The voice didn't belong to Ares, and I whirled back in time to see Dentro materialize from the forest around us. His bark-covered body was coiling around Ares, and his head flew low across the ground, stopping when he reached the fallen tooth. "You kept your word," he said, his rich voice soft. Green light flashed brightly at the same time as the twenty-foot tall God of War brought his sword crashing down onto Dentro's body.

The dragon hissed, retracting fast, whipping his serpentine tail through the trees around us, felling them all with an almighty crash. Ares had already lost interest in the dragon though, his awful eyes back on me.

I turned again to run, but stumbled as the pull on my power intensified. I didn't have enough power left. I likely only had minutes before I passed out, and then I would die. At Ares' hands. The thought was unbearable, and it felt as though all the love my heart had swelled with just minutes before was now acid, pouring through my body, toxic and cruel.

I felt something hard against my torso, and my vision blurred as I tried to fight against it.

"It is me, fierce one," Dentro's voice sounded in my head, and I stopped struggling as I was lifted from the ground.

I blinked through the rain, my breath catching and my heart almost stopping as Ares tore through the night, his sword as big as I was, and his face filled with murder. Dentro whipped me around, out of Ares' reach, his tail coiling tighter around me. I saw the dragon's wings snap out, massive and taut, through my hazy vision and with a blast of warm air, the creature leaped off the ground.

Ares let out another cry, this one filled with pure rage, as we moved higher. My head swam, then pain ripped through my gut, the cord connecting my power to Ares suddenly aflame within me. I screamed, unable to think or see, and Ares screamed louder below me. Then all of my power flooded back to me, and I opened my eyes, heaving for breath as everything around me sharpened and strengthened. Red covered my vision as it cleared, and suddenly I could see the forest getting smaller below me as we rose higher, the rain cold and hard.

"Take me back!"

"No. He will kill you."

"I am strong again, take me back!" I cried, struggling against the dragon's tail.

"You are strong again because you are too far away for him to take your power. If you go back, he will drain you, and kill you."

A strangled cry left my throat, and I beat my fist against Dentro's bark body. Desperation coursed through me, the pain inside my chest unbearable.

"I love him," I sobbed. "I can't leave him. I swore I wouldn't leave him again."

"I am sorry, fierce one. I can't take you back." The dragon's voice was filled with sorrow.

"What did she do to him? What did that fucking witch do? That's not him!"

"The Goddess of Love is a terrifying goddess to cross. But if you truly love Ares, I will help you lift the curse."

"I do. I do love him. I'll do anything. Please, we have to save him."

With another wracking sob, I let go of all the doubt, allowing the truth to wash over me completely as the dragon soared through the rain.

I loved Ares. And I would do anything to get him back.

THANKS FOR READING!

Thank you so much for reading The Savage God, I hope you enjoyed it! If so I would be very grateful for a review! They help so much; just click here and leave a couple words, and you'll make my day :)

You can order the next book, The Golden God, here.

You can also get exclusive first looks at artwork and story ideas, plus free short stories and audiobooks if you sign up to my newsletter at elizaraine.com.

CPSIA information can be obtained
at www.ICGtesting.com
Printed in the USA
LVHW090020240721
693518LV00003B/78